William Forrest

The History of Grisild the Second

A Narrative, in Verse, of the Divorce of Queen Katharine of Arragon

William Forrest

The History of Grisild the Second
A Narrative, in Verse, of the Divorce of Queen Katharine of Arragon

ISBN/EAN: 9783743418271

Manufactured in Europe, USA, Canada, Australia, Japa

Cover: Foto ©Andreas Hilbeck / pixelio.de

Manufactured and distributed by brebook publishing software (www.brebook.com)

William Forrest

The History of Grisild the Second

THE

Hiftory of Grifild the Second:

A NARRATIVE, IN VERSE, OF THE DIVORCE

OF QUEEN KATHARINE OF

ARRAGON.

WRITTEN BY WILLIAM. FORREST,

SOMETIME CHAPLAIN TO QUEEN MARY I.,

AND NOW EDITED, FOR THE FIRST TIME,

FROM THE AUTHOR'S MS. IN THE

BODLEIAN LIBRARY,

BY THE

REV. W. D. MACRAY, M.A., F.S.A.

LONDON:

PRINTED BY WHITTINGHAM AND .WILKINS,

AT THE CHISWICK PRESS.

1875.

The Roxburghe Club.

MDCCCLXXV.

TO

THE PRESIDENT AND MEMBERS OF

The Roxburghe Club,

THE HISTORY OF GRISILD THE SECOND,

(RESTORED FROM THE MS. IN THE BODLEIAN LIBRARY,)

IS DEDICATED AND PRESENTED BY THEIR

OBEDIENT SERVANT,

J. B. HEATH.

66, *Ruſſell Square.*

CONTENTS.

b

Preface.

HE poem now for the firſt time printed, is one which has been almoſt entirely overlooked by thoſe who have written on the important portion of Engliſh hiſtory to which it refers. Although its exiſtence has been known to the literary world by its being meñtioned by Wood, Tanner and Warton, and by a few ſhort extraćts occaſionally printed (as mentioned hereafter), it has nevertheleſs remained in undeſerved obſcurity. Little as it can claim of regard for poetical merit, there are yet a quaintneſs and a ſimplicity in the greater part of it that always redeem it from contempt, and often render it amuſing. But it is in the illuſtrations of contemporary hiſtory which it affords that its chief value lies. Freſh in perſonal knowledge of the events of which he writes, and of ſcenes of ſome of which he was an eye-witneſs, and enabled by official poſition as a royal chaplain to relate ſome things with ſpecial certainty, William Forreſt gives us here a record of the Great Divorce, which is ſecond

in date only to the eloquent proteſt of Cardinal Pole, contemporary with the narrative of Harpsfield,* and earlier than the hiſtories of Campian and Sanders, amongſt thoſe who eſpouſed the cauſe, as well as maintained the faith, of the rejeɛted Queen.

Of the perſonal hiſtory of this "ſymple Preeiſte," as he with ſufficient reaſon ſtyles himſelf, very little has as yet been aſcertained. We learn from himſelf that in the year 1530, when the King ſent to Oxford to procure the judgment of the Univerſity in his favour, he was then preſent at the diſcuſſions which enſued, "attending upon a certain good man" whoſe name he has unfortunately omitted. It is poſſible that he was himſelf a native of Oxford, ſince a family of the name of Foreſt was long ſettled there, as one of ſome little civic importance. In the records of the pariſhes of St. PeterintheEaſt and St. PeterleBailey, various perſons of the name of William Foreſt are met with between the years 1509 and 1600, and Dr. John Underhill, the third biſhop of Oxford during the reign of Queen Elizabeth,† was the ſon of the widow of one of theſe. We find from the Calendars of the State Papers that there were alſo ſeveral perſons bearing the ſame family name who were conneɛted with the Court. Edward Foreſt was Groom of the Chamber to Queen Katharine in 1517, and Miles Foreſt held the ſame office about the King, with whom he appears to have been in great favour;

* Nicholas Harpsfield's account of the divorce ſtill remains in MS. (in duplicate copies) in the library of New College, Oxford. A notice of it is appended to this Preface.

† MS. colleɛtions for the city of Oxford, by Mr. W. H. Turner, now transferred by him to the Bodleian Library.

while father John Forreft, Prior of Greenwich, and
Provincial of the Francifcans in England, who was
burned in 1538 for denying the King's Supremacy, was
Chaplain to Queen Katharine. Doubtlefs it was from
fome near relationfhip to thefe that our author obtained
his introduction at Court, and became fubfequently, as
we learn from himfelf that he did become, Chaplain to
Queen Mary. A fervant of the fame name was alfo
employed by Cardinal Wolfey, who probably claimed
kindred with the reft.*

That our author was an eye-witnefs of the erection of
Wolfey's College upon the fite of the Priory of S.
Fridefwide, is evident from the way in which he defcribes the "loitering," from the lack of good overfeers,
of the thoufand workmen thereon employed. And that
he was appointed to fome poft in the College as re-
founded by the King, appears from the occurrence of
his name amongft the penfioned members after its
diffolution, as the recipient of an annual allowance of
£6, in 1553 and 1556.† That he was prefent at the

---

* It may even be that as our author became a member of Cardinal
College, either on its original or on its fecond and regal foundation,
that he himfelf was the retainer of its Founder, but, if fo, that gratitude
which has been defined as "the expectation of benefits to come," left
him free after the fall of his mafter to fpeak of him in the fame terms
as does Sanders, and almoft in the language of Roy or Skelton. The
only mention of the name of Foreft found in the early regifters at Chrift
Church, occurs in the "Dean's entrance-book," where there is the
entry of a commoner fo named (whofe Chriftian name is not given),
under date of May, 1555. (Information of Rev. T. V. Bayne, M.A.)

† When this penfion ceafed to be paid has not been as yet afcer-
tained. The Iffue Roll of the Exchequer for the 9th year of Elizabeth
(1566-7) being the firft roll of her reign now remaining in the Public

funeral of Queen Katherine at Peterborough, in 1536, is fhown by his recital of details which are not preferved, it is believed, by any other writer. In 1548 we find him dedicating his verfion of the treatife *De regimine principum* to the Duke of Somerfet, as alfo in 1551 his paraphrafes of fome of the Pfalms. This continued choice of patron, together with the character of the latter work, gives fome reafon for Warton's fufpicion "that our author could accommodate his faith to the reigning powers."* A further and a ftrong corrobora- tion of this is found in the curious fact that while in the poem before us he inveighs ftrongly (at p. 67) againft Dr. Cox, the Chancellor of Oxford, for perfecuting all clergy and "religious" who continued to wear their fhaven crowns, he yet, at the beginning of his treatife on the *Governance of Princes*, reprefents himfelf in a neat drawing as a rather young man, with fome- what oftentatioufly full and flowing hair, in the attitude of prefenting his book to the Protector. But in 1553 we find him, on the other hand, coming forward with warm congratulations on the acceffion of the new and reactionary fovereign.

Among Browne Willis's MS. collections for Bucking- hamfhire preferved in the Bodleian Library, double entries are found of the prefentation of William Foreft by Anthony Lamfon, on July 1, 1556, to the Vicarage of Bledlow, in that county. In Lipfcomb's *Hiftory of*

Record Office,—a bulky record of enormous length,—has been kindly examined for the Editor by his friend Mr. H. Gough, with the negative refult of afcertaining that Forreft's name does not occur there.

* *Hift. of Englifh Poetry*, fect. 53.

Buckinghamſhire, the name of the preſentee is given as
William *Forteſcue*. As the county was then in the
dioceſe of Lincoln, the epiſcopal regiſter which contains
the record of the preſentation is conſequently preſerved
at Lincoln, and it has not been poſſible for the Editor
to make a ſearch there, and clear up the diſcrepancy.*
In 1558 Forreſt preſents to his royal miſtreſs the poem
here printed, which he tells us was completed on the
25th of June. Of his fortunes after her deceaſe we
know nothing, except that from the faʤ of his dedicating his *Hiſtory of Joſeph* to Thomas Howard, Duke of
Norfolk, ſhortly before that nobleman's execution in
1572, we may conjeʤure that he found a refuge, under
the again-altered ſtate of things, in the proteʤion of that
ſtaunch adherent of the unreformed religion. And that
Forreſt himſelf then remained in the ſame faith to the
laſt, may be gathered from the faʤ that all that we know
further about him is that the two dates of "27 Oʤ.
1572, per me Guil. Forreſtum" and "1581", occur,
the one at the end and the other at fol. 95 of a volume
(Harl. MS. 1703) containing a poem which treats of
the Life of the Bleſſed Virgin and of the Immaculate
Conception, in the ſpirit of a moſt devout adorer, as
well as other controverſial verſes. But in religion,

* As B. Willis uſed the Lincoln Regiſters, it is, however, probable
that he has taken his own entry from them. In reply to a letter
addreſſed to the Vicar of Bledlow, with the enquiry whether any
pariſh records exiſt which might give the true name, the Editor has
been informed that the Regiſters do not reach back further than to
1592. If our author was really the perſon preſented, his penſion probably ceaſed on the promotion. The next incumbent of the pariſh was
appointed in 1576.

although Roman, he was not Papal; he fhared that
old Englifh diflike to the ufurped domination of the
Bifhop of Rome, which fo largely helped to the general
acceptance of the high-handed meafures of Henry VIII.
In one of his poems in the Harleian MS. he fpeaks
ftrongly of the right of each national branch of the
Church to enjoy felf-government, and of each Bifhop to
rule his own diocefe, relegating by name the Bifhop of
Rome to his own fee.* The right ufe of relics is treated
of with great moderation in his *Hiftory of Jofeph.*

Apart from theological views, Forreft often dif-
plays in his various writings great good feeling and
good fenfe, with a ftrong love of juftice and fair dealing.
This is particularly fhown in his *Hiftory of Jofeph* and
the *Governance of Princes,* where there is much on the
management of fervants, the condition of the poor, and
the raifing of rents, which is full of intereft, and affords
curious illuftrations of the times.

In the poem before us, its fimplicity and ruggednefs,
through which nothing in the narrative is facrificed to
elegance of diction (the author himfelf telling us, at p.
133, that he regards truth more than accuracy of metre),
render its hiftorical illuftrations the more interefting and
truftworthy. In addition to the points to which the
few notes appended to this volume refer, other matters
deferving notice are, the diftinct ftatement of the merce-
nary views of Henry VII. in regard to his fon's marriage with the widowed Katharine; † the defcription of

* See Appendix, p. 187.
† The Simancas State Papers (calendared as yet only to the year
1526), afford full confirmation of the miferable money-getting aims

Katharine's perfonal appearance, and of her devotion and alms-deeds; * the notices of the charaĉter of Henry VIII., depiĉted with great apparent fairnefs, and the account of the proceedings in Oxford at the Convocations about the divorce.†

which influenced Henry VII. They fhow that after the death of Prince Arthur, he aĉtually at firft propofed to marry Katharine himfelf; a propofal which, however, affords ftrong prefumptive evidence that her marriage had never been confummated. They fhow alfo that, in her early Englifh days, fhe was far too much influenced by a young Confeffor, of immoral charaĉter, Fray Diego Fernandez, againft whom the Spanifh ambaffadors themfelves conftantly protefted, and who was at laft judicially difmiffed about the year 1515. Mr. Bergenroth believes that thefe letters contain imputations on the honour of Katharine herfelf; but the idea feems very far from being borne out by the documents themfelves, while it is contradiĉted by the whole hiftory of her life; and if it were correĉt, we may be fure that Henry VIII. would not have hefitated in after years to have availed himfelf of the evidence which would have been forthcoming. We learn from the Preface, by Don Pafcual de Gayangos, to the firft part of vol. iii. of the Calendar of thefe State Papers (1873, p. x.), that there is in the Library of the Efcurial, a hiftory of Henry VIII. from 1530, with part of the reign of Edward VI., written by a Spanifh lawyer who came to England in Katharine's fuite, which is "full of interefting details."

    * "Seeleden is feene Prynceffe the pooare to vifyte
        And with her owne handys the fame tapparayle."—(P. 145.)
In our own days this rare fight is happily not infrequently reproduced in the aĉts of our own Queen.

    † The corruption and intimidation that were employed on the King's fide are well known. The amufing but very doubtful ftory told in Wood's *Hiftory of Oxford* (vol. ii. p. 46, 1796), of a regentmafter of Balliol College, who bore the very apocryphal name of King Henry, rufhing to vote at a convocation held clandeftinely at midnight, againft the divorce, with his breeches thrown haftily over his fhoulders inftead of a hood, and for which Wood only gives as a reference "Anon. MS.," is taken from a MS. in his own colleĉtion now in the Bodleian Library, D. 18, entitled, "Apology for the Government of the Univerfity, againft Hen. VIII. 1597."

c

The frequent ufe of proverbs and proverbial expref-
fions is a charaƈteriftic of the fimplicity of Forreft's
ftyle, as it was of the ftyle of his friend Alex. Barclay, the tranflator of Brandt's *Ship of Fools*, of whom
(fcantily noticed by contemporaries*) he gives fome
interefting particulars which will be found in the
Appendix to this volume. A lift of thofe which occur
in the prefent poem, and of fome which have been
noticed in his *Hiftory of Jofeph*, is fubjoined in the note
below.† In his fpelling, Forreft conftantly doubles in
a rather unufual manner the vowels *e* and *o*, and in
words ending in *ew* or *ue*, generally tranfpofes thefe
two letters, writing *knwe*, *nwe*, *rwe*, *dwe*, for *knew*, *new*,
rue, *due*, &c. He alfo almoft invariably places an acute

* See Mr. T. H. Jamiefon's " Life of Barclay," prefixed to his
edition of Barclay's *Ship of Fools*, p. lxxxii. 4to. Edinb. 1874.
† " Man proponeth, God difpofeth," p. 33.
" To pick a thank," p. 49.
" Two wits better than one," p. 51.
" To have an oar in a thing," p. 54.
" Like a dog with a burnt tail," p. 58.
" The glover faid the dog was mad, in order to have his fkin," p. 81.
" Inter pontem et fontem," p. 123 [" Mifericordia Domini inter
pontem et.fontem ;" a faying afcribed to S. Auguftine].
" Happy the brood in which there is neither thief nor unthrift,"
p. 156.
" Had I wift," p. 158.
" Bleffed are they that live in reft," *ibid.*
" To draw by one ftring," p. 159.
In the *Jofeph* thefe are met with amongft others :—
" To kifs the poft," p. 172.
" Let him that is cold blow the coal," p. 172.
" The young cock crows after the old," p. 177.
" Thou fhalt fcace know the moone from a greene cheefe."
" A newe broome fweeapeth bothe fayre and cleane."

accent over the article *a*, and occafionally over that letter
at the commencement of a word.

Warton (*Hiſt. Poet.*) defcribes Forreſt as being
"eminently ſkilled in muſic," and fays, that "with
much diligence and expenfe he collected the works of
the moſt excellent Englifh compofers that were his
contemporaries." His love and knowledge of Church
muſic may be inferred from the paſſage at p. 141,
where he fays that no fuch "melodious fong" was
heard throughout the world as was heard in England,
from the mention of his own performance of divine
fervice at p. 186, and from his notice of the Proteſtant
compofer, whilom his friend, on the fame page.* But
the only pofitive evidence of which the editor is aware,
is afforded by the MS. in the Library of the Muſic
School at Oxford, which Warton mentions. It is a
collection of eighteen Maſſes, in ſix parts, and confequently in ſix volumes, in oblong quarto, written by
two hands. In the counter-tenor book is the following infcription :—" William Forreſt hunc librum juræ
(*ſic*) poſſidet, cum quinque aliis eidem pertinentibus ;"
the date of 1530 has been added by a later hand.† The
volumes are bound in black calf, ſtamped in double com-
partments, bearing—1, The arms of England, with the
dragon and greyhound as fupporters, and in the upper
corners the fun and moon, and ſhields with croſſes; 2,

* Probably this was John Taverner, of whom Fuller fays (*Church
Hiſt.*, cent. xvi. p. [171].) that he repented of having fet fo many Popifh
ditties to muſic.

† Burney MS. 357 (Brit. Mus.) written in the eleventh or twelfth
century, formerly " Liber Sancte Marie de Thame," bears alfo Forreſt's
name as owner : " Liber Gulielmi Forreſti."

The Tudor rofe, fupported by angels, and with the pomegranate (the badge of Katharine of Arragon) below, furrounded by the motto,—

" Hec rofa virtutis de celo miffa fereno
Eternū florens regia fceptra feret." *

It would appear from this binding that Forreſt had obtained thefe volumes from the royal library.

It now only remains to defcribe the MS. from which this volume is taken, and to enumerate the other extant writings of its author.

The *Hiſtory of Grifilde the Seconde*† exiſts amongſt the MSS. of Ant. à Wood in the Bodleian Library, No. 2 of that collection which was bought by the Univerfity after his death. It is evidently the copy prefented by the author to Queen Mary, being beautifully written on fine vellum,‡ and having been originally " bound in laced

---

* This motto, found on the binding of many of the King's books, appears to have been afterwards adapted to Anne Boleyn, by the addition of a monogram of the letters AH.| The Bodleian Library poſſeſſes a Salluſt, printed in 1519, which bears on its covers the arms of England, impaling thofe of Caſtile, Leon, Arragon, Sicily and Granada, on one fide, and thofe of England alone on the other. It may poſſibly have been ufed by Mary as one of her fchool-books. Many Engliſh and Latin words are interlined in the text in two or three contemporary hands; and a few of thefe interlineations bear fome refemblance to the handwriting of her father.

† In the fcheme of education drawn up in 1523 by Jo. Lud. Vives for the ufe of the Queen in the training of her daughter, the "Grefilida vulgata jam fabula" was one of the very few ſtories fanctioned as fit for perufal (Madden's *Privy Purfe Expenfes of P. Mary*, 1831, p. cxxiv.) It is curious that this ſtory of Patient Grifild fhould thus afterwards have been taken as the type of the life of Katharine.

‡ Proper names occurring in the poem are written in red ink; thefe are here printed in italics, but other rubricated words, which frequently occur, have not been thus diftinguiſhed.

fatin." Nearly all the lace has now difappeared, and the fatin is tattered and faded. It has clafps, and brafs boffes with the words " Ave Maria, gracia plēa " at each corner, as well as a centre bofs. It formerly belonged to Ralph Sheldon of Wefton Park, Warwick-fhire, who gave it to his friend Wood. Wood extraĉted fome paffages in his Englifh Annals of the Univerfity of Oxford, being the accounts of the Convocations about the divorce and of the doings of Dean Cox of Ch. Ch. (pp. 75-79 and 66-68 *infra*) which are printed in Gutch's edition of the *Annals* (1796) vol. ii., pp. 47-49 and 115-117. The whole of the ninth chapter was con-tributed by Dr. Blifs in 1814 to vol. iv. of Sir E. Brydges' *Britifh Bibliographer*, where it occupies pp. 200-5. Dr. Blifs alfo printed the firft three ftanzas of the *Oration Confolatory* in the account of Forreft given in his edition of Wood's *Athenæ*, vol. i. col. 300. And Sir F. Madden printed the firft five ftanzas of chap. iv., refpeĉting the education of Mary, in his Preface to Mary's *Privy Purfe Expenfes*, p. cxix. With thefe few exceptions the whole of the poem has hitherto remained inedited.

Forreft's other known poetical works are as follows:—

I. *The Hiftory of Jofeph the Chaifte compofed in balladde royall crudely* ; largely derived from the Teftaments of the Twelve Patriarchs. In two parts: the firft, contain-ing the ftory of Jofeph's adverfity, in forty-feven chap-ters ; the fecond, containing his profperity, in forty-two chapters. Dedicated to Thomas Howard, Duke of Norfolk, and dated as having been finifhed 11th April, 1569, but faid by the author to have been originally

written twenty-four years before. A copy on vellum
in two volumes folio was in the poffeffion of Mr. Charles
Theyer in 1697, being numbered 243, 244 in the lift of
his MSS. in Bernard's *Cat. MSS. Angliæ.* He fhowed
Wood one volume in 1680, and told* him he intended
to give it to Univerfity College Library. This intention
was carried out before 1700, and in the library of that
College the firft part remains, handfomely bound in
tooled calf with corner boffes.† The fecond part is now
(together with others of Theyer's MSS.) in the Royal
Library, Britifh Mufeum, 18. C. xiii., bound in a more
recent covering of vellum. Another perfeᷭt copy of the
work, containing both parts in one folio volume of 286
pages written on paper, is in the poffeffion of Rev. J. E.
A. Fenwick, at Thirleftane Houfe, Cheltenham, being
in the vaft colleᷭtion of MSS. of the late Sir Thomas
Phillipps, which that gentleman has inherited. At the
end it has the initials of an old owner, E. B., with
the Welfh motto (the motto of the families of Meredyth
and Moftyn), "Heb Dhuw, heb dhim." In 1693 it was
in the poffeffion of the Earl of Stamford; afterwards in
that of Thomas Lloyd, Efq., at whofe fale in July,
1819, it was purchafed by Mr. Heber for £20 10s.; at
Heber's fale in February, 1836, (part xi. p. 80, No.
796), it was purchafed by Thorpe, the bookfeller, for
the fmall fum of £6 16s. 6d., in whofe catalogue of
MSS. in 1836 it is defcribed, and who fold it finally to
Sir Thomas Phillipps for £12 12s. This copy appears

* Wood MS. D. 18.
† For free ufe of this MS. the Editor is indebted to the courtefy of
A. Chavaffe, Efq., the Librarian.

to contain fome additions to the other; in part i. there
is a curious chapter comparing a Welfh lady (noted in
the margin as being Anne Vavafer, wife of Andrew
Vavafer, whofe paramour was one Richard Parry,) to
Potiphar's wife, Memphytica, with notices of her pride
and evil manners; and at the end of the volume there
is an addrefs to all claffes of perfons urging the perufal
of the book for the leffons which it contains. At the
end of the dedication to the Duke of Norfolk (who
was beheaded in 1572), there is this note in red ink,—
" Of this Dukes myferable fall fhortlye after the de-
lyverye of this Booke, looke at thende of this fame";
but thofe, however, who look, find nothing.*

II. A verfion and variation of the treatife called
Ariftotle's, but really written by Ægidius Romanus
towards the end of the thirteenth century, entitled *De
regimine principum.* This was written in 1548, and
dedicated, as before mentioned, to the Duke of Somerfet,
but intended, when fanctioned by him, for the ufe of
Edward VI. A copy on vellum, in quarto, containing
feventy-eight leaves, is in the Royal Library, Brit. Mus.
17 D. III. The additions made by Forreft himfelf contain much of very great intereft.

III. A metrical verfion of fome of the Pfalms;
written in 1551, and alfo dedicated to the Duke of
Somerfet, with a high panegyric on Sternhold. A paper
MS. in octavo, Royal Libr. Brit. Mus., 17 A. XXI.
This appears to be the MS. formerly in Weftminfter

---

* The Editor defires to exprefs his obligations to Mr. Fenwick for
kindly permitting him to examine this volume.

Abbey, No. 225, which is defcribed in Bernard's Catalogue in 1697 as " Some Pfalms in Englifh verfe, by
W. Foreft," but which is no longer to be found there.
The Pfalms here verfified are, 6—20, 22, 23, 25, 30, 32,
35, 37, 42, 45—47, 52, 53, 55, 56, 59, 60, 65, 66, 69,
71, 74, 85, 87, 92, 94, 95—97, 100, 112, 129, 148,
150, together with the *Te Deum, Benedictus, Magnificat*,
and *Nunc Dimittis*. Out of thefe forty-nine, fifteen had
been previoufly paraphrafed by Sternhold in his collection of thirty-feven Pfalms printed in 1549. In the
MS. noticed under the next head, there are alfo verfions
of Pfalms 1—6, 8, 11—13.

IV. Life of the Bleffed Virgin Mary; a poem in
praife of her, and in honour of the Immaculate Conception; followed by mifcellaneous moral and religious
verfes; dated from 1572 to 1581. Harleian MS. 1703,
a folio volume on paper. On the fly-leaf is written
" W. Foreft's Poems to Q. Mary." This is the title
given in Bernard's Catalogue in 1697 to No. 44 of the
MSS. then in the poffeffion of Henry Worfeley, of
Lincoln's Inn. It feems, moreover, that this is the
volume defcribed in Wood's *Athenæ*, as having been
in the poffeffion of the Earl of Ailefbury.* It has the
fame motto and initials on the firft leaf as the Phillipps
MS. of the *Jofeph*, " Heb Dhuw heb dhim. E. B."

V. *A new Ballade of the Marigolde. Imprinted at
London in Alderfgate Street by Richard Lant.* Verfes on

---

* Some theological and controverfial treatifes, apparently in profe,
are alfo there enumerated as being in the Earl's poffeffion, which have
not as yet been further traced.

the acceffion of Queen Mary: figned with Forreft's name. Fourteen ftanzas of eight lines.

A copy of the original broadfide is in the library of the Society of Antiquaries at Burlington Houfe; and it was reprinted by Thomas Park in vol. x. of the fecond edition of the *Harleian Mifcellany*, 4to. Lond. 1813, p. 253.

VI. *Pater Nofter* and *Te Deum*, verfified as a Prayer and a Thankfgiving for Queen Mary. Thefe are only found in the firft edition of Foxe's *Acts and Monuments*, printed in 1563, pp. 1139-40, and have never been re-printed in any fubfequent edition. Foxe thus introduces them:—" And for fo much as prayer is here mencioned for Quene Mary, here folowethe to be fene the Pater Nofter then fette forth in Englifhe meter, compiled or rather corrupted by one W. Foreft.

    *   *   *   *   *

> *The Pater Nofter to gods glory,*
>   *with prayer to him for Qyene Mary,*
> Our father which in heauen dofte ·fit
>   We fanctifie thy name,
> Our praier we praye thee to admyt,
>   Quene Mary faue from blame."
>   [&c. Six more quatrains.]

" *Te deum, lauding God fpecially,*
>   *with prayer therin for our Qyene Mary.*
> O God thy name we magnifie,
>   In thy fanctuary,
> For that thou haft of thy mercy
>   Sent us our Quene Mary.

To thee this all our Englifhe grounde
Doth render prayfe alway :
Whome mercyfull hath euer founde,
So healpe vs ftyll we praye." [&c. 116 lines more.]

As thefe compofitions both end with the formula,
" Finis, quod W. F.," they were probably printed as
broadfides, like the preceding poem.

With thefe the lift of Forreft's known poems con-
cludes; poems which, however profaic under the form
of verfe, are all of them full of intereft, alike as illuftrations of the hiftory and manners of his times, and as
illuftrations of language. Under both afpeéts it is believed that this volume will be found to deferve no
little regard.

DUCKLINGTON RECTORY, OXON.,
May 29, 1875.

Note to Page xii.

Nicholas Harpsfield's Treatife concerning Marriage, occafioned by
the Divorce of Q. Katharine (New Coll. MS. 311.)
In Three Books.

Book I.—Certain Reafons and Arguments to juftify the Marriage,
with an Abftract of a book written in Latin by Bp. Fifher, " and never
yett printed fo farre as wee knowe," in anfwer to the book printed in
England, both in Latin and Englifh, in defence of the cenfures of the
Univerfities.

Book II.—Anfwers to (i.) Egidius de Bella Mera, " that long before
our tyme writeth of this matter ;" (ii.) Marcus Mantua, " a learned lawyer of Padua and one of our owne tyme ;" (iii.) a little Latin book of
Mr. Robert Wakefield, one of the King's chaplains, againft Bp. Fifher,
printed (there is alfo extant " fome booke of his which I have not
feene"); (iv.) an anonymous dialogue in Englifh called " The Glafs of
Truth." With an hiftorical difcourfe of the Divorce, and the contents
of certain letters fent by the King and Cardinal Wolfey to the King's
agents at Rome.

Book III.—Difcourfes on the Acts of Parliament about the divorces
of Katharine, Anne Boleyn, and Anne of Cleves, fhewing the repug-
nance of the fame to the book made in defence of the divorce of the
firft, and the manifold plagues that fell afterwards on the King's mar-
riages and on the whole realm. [This book includes a vindication of
Sir Thomas More.]

The treatife was written during the reign of Q. Mary (f. 302).

Interefting extracts about Q. Katharine's manner of life and habits
of devotion while at Buckden, and the refults of the diffolution of abbeys,
are printed by Hearne at pp. 640-645 of his Gloffary to Langtoft's Chron-
icle. The account of the fecret marriage with Anne Boleyn, printed in

Latin by Le Grand (*Hift. du Divorce,* &c., 1688, vol. ii. pp. 109-111.) from an anonymous MS. narrative, and which has been quoted from him by all later hiftorians, is here found almoft *verbatim* in Englifh (ff. 244-5.) There are curious anecdotes (amongft others) of the licking up by a dog of the blood from the body of Henry VIII. before his embalming (in fulfilment of a warning uttered by Peto, the Obfervant Friar, in his famous fermon before the king), as reported by one William Confell, who faid he was there prefent, and with much ado drove away the dog (f. 209); and of Cranmer's being nominated Archbifhop of Canterbury when attending upon the King at a bear-baiting (f. 308ᵇ.), as alfo of his carrying his wife about with him concealed in a great cheft full of holes, for which cheft on the occafion of a fire at his palace in Canterbury all other care was fet afide, the archbifhop crying out that it contained his evidences and other writings which he efteemed above any worldly treafure : "this I heard out of the mouth of a gentleman that was there prefent." (f. 291ᵇ.) A fimilar verfion of the ftory of the dog is extraᵭed in Hearne's Gloffary to Langtoft, p. 560, from Hall's *Life of Bifhop Fifher,* printed in 1655.

Gryſilde the Seconde.

[PROLOGUE.]

To the moſte excellente and vertuous Prynces, oure moſte
gratious ſoueraigne ladye, Marye (by the grace of God)
Queene of Englande, France, Naples, Hieruſalem, and
Irelande, Defendreſſe of the faith, Prynceſſe of Spaine, and
Cicilie, Archeducheſſe of Auſtria, Ducheſſe of Millayne,
Burgundye, and Brabande, Counteſſe of Haſpurge, Flaun-
dres, & Tyrale, Youre maieſties moſte faithefull, louynge
& obedyent Subieɛte, William Forreſte, wiſcheth all grace
and fauour from God aboue, longe life (yn goode healthe) and
proſperous reigne : withe (after this life) æternall felicitee.

¶ The Prologe *to* the *Queenis* Maieſtee.

S Nature hathe an inclynation
    Unto the lyvely louinge parent ;
    So, younge humayne propagation
    To heeare recordys of their freendys
      auncyent,
    Their aɛtys recomptinge that weare
      excellent,
Thoughe not ſo of the contraryous ſorte,
Bycauſe no renowne their fame dothe reporte.

The naturall
childe delitethe
the goode re-
porte of the
parent.

B

To thende, he ſeruynge God, the childe may doo the lyke.
What more renowne to childe redounde maye,.
Then as to reade or heeare, by recomptinge,
Howe his parentys in their lyuynge daye ·
Had heere God in highe reuerencinge,
His honour, ſeruice, and lawes mayntayninge,
That hee, not degeneratinge thearfro,
May (in his lyuynge) practice the like ſo.

The parentys euyll example the chylde ought tauoyde
Or, whoe dothe reade or heeare the contrarye,
His parentys to bee nocyuous and yll,
But that it maye geue motyon ynwardelye
As to beeware the like to fulfyll.
Bothe are to bee knowne: *Paule* graunteth thear till,
omnia probate, quod bonum eſt tenete [1] Theſſalo. [v. 21.]
After the goode oure wayes to dyrecte,
All euyl examples for to rejecte.

Filius non portabit iniquitatem patris, niſi, ut pater, inſequitur proles.
Vnknowne it is not to men of knowledge
But parentys hathe beene, ſome peruerſe, ſome goode :
The badde, the childe ſhall not his doingis pledge,
Or anſweare thearfore withe trobled moode,
Except as parent ſo ſuethe the broode ;
Then, withe the like, for like myſgouernaunce,
Awarded they bee, by Dyuyne ordynaunce.

Filius ſapiens, gloria patris. [Prov. x. 1.] As the towardys chylde a joye to the father, ſo the goode father joye to the chylde.
If vertuous younge impe, wyttie and towardys,
To parent á pleaſure and glorye bee,
And, contrarye wiſe, the peruerſe and frowardys
Annoyaunce and greate infelicitee,
Semblable wiſe then, maye ſerue in degree
The godly parent the chylde to reioyce,
Bycawſe the beſte waies hee tooke heere in choyce.

Howe muche (O noble and excellent Queene !)
Maye then delyte youre domynation
Youre Mothers meeke life of youe to bee feene,
Or reduced to commemoration,
That was of mofte worthye commendation,
Perfectely knowne to hundreadys that yeat bee,
As mofte efpecyall to youre maieftee.

Howe ought to
reioice our
noble Queene
the lyfe to
reade of her
mofte godlye
Mother.

Well I confydre at this prefent daye
No fewe hathe tawlke of her highe worthynes,
Howe vnto vertue fhe gaue her alwaye,
And deadys of pytee paffinglye doubtles,
Witheftandinge her enemye, for all his ftowtnes,
The fathanyke Serpent, whoe had her in hate,
But neauer cowlde her (to his purpofe) culpate.

The vertues of
noble queene
Catharyne are
remembred at
this prefent
daye.

For that fhe was fo fpeciall notable,
In this inconftant mofte daungerous tyme,
(—Whiche to adnote is muche myferable,
As maye bee exprefte in profe or in ryme,
Concordinge withe oure firft mateir, the flyme,
Whiche as it is muche lothefome and fylthie,
So all earthelye our practycingis gyltie ;—)

For fhe was
fo fpeciall
gratious, her
life the wor-
thier to be put
in recordis.

I thought it goode for reformation,
By her examples to vertues increafe,
Wheare reftethe gohoftelye inclynation,
To prompte them withe this in á readynes,
As rule to induce to all godlynes,
Thus muche to that ende feruynge the rather
For that in knowledge the fame wee gather.

Her life may
be as rule
others lyues
in vertue
to dyrecte.

While ſhe was ſet by, this Royalme floriſched, but not ſo afterwardes.

Well ought her holye conuerſation
Heere, in this Royalme, bee put in remembraunce,
For, while ſhe was in digne eſtymation,
It floriſcht in wealthe, and all abundaunce
That ſpeciallye ſerued to mannys ſuſtynaunce,
Withe of Goddys lawe bothe awe and reuerence,
And nowe fallen into great inconuenyence,

Errour and couetouſnes entred this Royalme after her depoſition.

As into erroure moſte ſpecyallye
By Schiſmys and Sectys, of Sathans owne rayſinge,
Withe Couetouſnes vniuerſallye,
To ſundry (the pooarys) vtter vndoinge,
Due Obedyence raſchelye contempnynge ;
Theis, withe hundreadys of myſeryes mo,
Hathe entred ſithe ſhee was reiected ſo.

This Royalme plaged for ſynnes accuſtome, ſpronge from the cheif.

Whiche I impute a plage of punyſchement
By all examples of antiquytee,
For ſynnes accuſtome moſte worthelye ſent,
Engendred from the highe nobilytee,
And ſpredde ouer all by muche fragilytee,
Whiche (I heere ſaye) may well bee veryfied,
Her holy life myght in nowiſe abyde,

This warke is but as a ſparke in comparaſon of her whoale lyfe.

As appearethe in this narration,
Compacte, in forte as oure knowledge dothe leade,
And with others auxiliation,
That muche in the ſame did vs alſo ſteade ;
Whoe that voucheſauethe, the ſame for to reade ;
Thoughe oure ſaide traueyle, in this preſent warke,
To her whoale life is but as a ſmall ſparke ;

Directinge the fame to youre maieftee
As to her onlye, and dearefte of all,
Not of purpofe, or meere neceffitee,
Her hereby vnto remembraunce to call,
And els (witheoute this) not fo to bee fall,
But, as yee and the godlye dothe the fame,
So, oure pofterytee to heeare of her fame.

*This warke
(as to her chef-
eft jewell) di-
rected to our
Queenys
maieftie.*

Her I heere lyken to *Gryfilde* the goode,
As well I fo maye, for her great patience ;
Confyderinge althingis withe her howe it ftoode,
Her geauynge that name theare is none offenfe ;
Your noble Father workinge like pretence
As *Walter* to *Gryfilde*, by muche vnkyndenes,
By name of *Walter* I dooe hym expreffe.

*By names
Gryfilde and
Walter our
Queenys
Father and
Mother ex-
amplyfyed.*

Whiche noble Father, I cannot but faye,
Was leadde in fome parte by meanys of the light ; *
Perhaps for fynne, that reigned at that daye,
God fuffred this Royalme fo to alter quyte,
Or for that He wolde fhewe His dyuyne myght,
Hable terecte by the weake and frayle fex,
Howe eauer Sathan His Churche did heere vex ;

*Oure Kynge
fomewhat
ledde by the
counfell of
vndifcreeit
perfons.*

Or, peraduenture, Hee wolde it bee fo
To trye (in meekenes) her ftabilitee,
In higher meryte to haue her to go,
For to alaye heere her fragilite ;
In quyet eftate fhewthe not humylite
To eauerlaftinge remuneration,
As in troble and tyme of temptation.

*In quyet eftate
humylite is not
tryed as yn
the tyme of
temptation.*

---

* [*i. e.* by means of light perfons.]

For oughtes heere wry-tinge amyſſe this Author humbly deſy-reth perdon.

Such my concepte, conceaved in this thinge ;
If from yoüre pleaſure it ſwerue anye waye
Youre gratious perdon I crave on kneis knelinge
Before (in readinge) my fawte me bewraye ;
Commendinge your grace bothe by night and daye,
Meanynge to Hym, bothe wakinge and ſleepinge,
That hathe your Mothers ſweete ſowle in keepinge.

¶ The Table.

*A table directinge to the chëif and principall poyntis of this
Booke by ordre of Chapiters, as after enfuethe.*

¶ *Caput* 1.

O what ende wryters endeauorethe their paynes.
¶ This hiftorye of *Grifilde the feconde* wryten
to this ende, other (of meekenes) to take
thearby fruyte.

¶ Of *Father* and *Mother*, and what noble howfe was
iffued this younge ladye *Gryfilidis*.

¶ Of her education and wondreful towardnes yn her
youthe to all godlynes and vertue.

¶ Howe, emongys all vertues, fhe embraced humylitee.

¶ A breeue defcription of her complexion and perfonage.

¶ Howe, tavoyde all infolent and light inwarde motions,
fhe gaue herfelfe much to contemplatife life.

¶ Howe (voydinge idlenes) fhe oftetymes wolde practice
withe the nedyll, and other handye bufineffies, to ladies
neceffarye.

¶ Euery moarnynge, and at nyght, twoe howres (at the
leafte) vpon her kneeis in her chambre or clofett
occupyinge herfelfe in godlye prayer.

¶ To riche and pooare ſhe ſhewed alwaies benynge
cheare, readye to dooe her deauer in all godlye aſſayes.

¶ She euermore endeauoringe the glorye of God, deteſt-
ing (as deathe) all worldely praiſes and vaine glorye.

¶ The vertuous vp tradinge of youthe attendinge vpon
her, whois Cowrte was as it had beene religious.

¶ Howe nothinge ſhe wanted of princely behauyour,
nurture, and ſuche, to womanlynes appertaynynge.

¶ All her life was geauen to godlynes, by ſpeciall grace
which God did her indue.

¶ Caput 2.

¶ The worthie fame of this noble *Gryſilde* blowne into
greate *Britaine*, was, by the kinge theare, (called the
ſeconde *Salomon*) procured ·in mariage to his eldeſt
ſunne.

¶ After the deſpouſaile, within ſhorte ſpace, withoute
knowledge of her huſbonde, ſhe became wydowe, and
of her lamentable heauynes and ſorowinges for hym.

¶ In her great heauynes for her huſbonde (ymputinge
herſelfe moſte infortunate) ſhe commendethe her
whoalye to Goddis ordynaunce, his takinge awaye (by
deathe) to bee as a plage for her iniquitee.

¶ Caput 3.

¶ The kinge (*Gryſildis* father in lawe) by aſſent of all
Chriſtian clergie, and the Popis then witheall, mar-
ryethe her to his other ſunne (*Walter*).

¶ The kinge ſhortelye dyethe; *Walter* is crowned Kinge
and *Gryſilde* alſo Queene moſte honorablye.

¶ A prynce was borne betweene this noble *Walter* and *Grifilde*, which not longe heere contynued lief.

¶ After muche forrowinge of *Grifilde* for her childe, how fhe (mofte wyttelye) appeaced the fame, not contraryinge Goddis ordynaunce, whome (well fhe wifte) at his dyvyne pleafure myght fende her like fruyte as He did that.

¶ God (remembringe his fervaunte *Walter*) fendethe hym by *Gryfilde* his wife a nwe fayre increafe, a doughter, havynge to name *Marye*.

¶ *Caput* 4.

¶ Of *Grifildis* upp tradinge her younge goodly princes, of her fingular towardnes in all vertue, *Thomas Lynaker* her cheif inftructor in the Latyne tunge.

¶ In *Britayne* that feafon was muche quyetnes and plentye of all goode thingis, the honour of God florifcheinge, the riche mercyful, the pooare nurifched.

¶ Howe *Grifilde* had alwaies before her iyes the love of God, caftinge to pleafe Hym before all worldelye thingis.

¶ Of her large difpofinge her almys to the pooare, and fpeciallye to the aged, weake and ympotent.

¶ In townys wheare fhe came fhe ofte gave fhurtys, fmocks, and other neceffaryes to the pooare and neady.

¶ Sometymes fecreatlye fhe wolde vyfite the pooare lyinge in childe bedde, and leave theare behynde her bothe fheeatys, lynnen, and other neceffaryes, fpecially monay for candyll, fyer and fuche other neadfull thyngys.

c

¶ She was not quoyiſche, prowde or diſdaynefull, but coulde bee contented (for Chriſtis ſake) to viſite the pooare.

¶ Oftetymes wolde ſhe riſe at myddnyght, and ſerve God in prayer, (as the Religious dyd), and devout contemplation.

¶ Thoughe this goode *Gryſilde* weare lyvynge in this worlde, yeat in the ſame ſhe had no delyte but in the worlde to come.

¶ For the devotion ſhe ſpecially had to the Paſſion of Chriſte, ſhee let make an Image repreſentinge the ſame, of wondrefull woorkemanſhippe, a lyttle from London, neeare to the waye goinge to Iſyllingeton.

¶ Howe, above all nàtyons, ſhe loved an Engliſcheman, doinge for dyverſe of them manye ſundrye benefyciall deadys, and ſhèe (to all goode) in ſyngular acceptation.

¶ Wheareeaver ſhe became, the people moſte hartely wolde praye for her grace, commendinge her aſmuch as they wolde *Walter* their kynge.

¶ This noble *Griſilde* was ſpeciall benyficiall in mayntaynynge of Scholars to learnynge, bothe in *Oxforde* and alſo in *Cambrydge*.

¶ *Caput* 5.

¶ How, at the Dyvyllis (and certayne of his) inſtigation, *Walter* ſought meanys to bee dyvorſed from *Griſilde*, for that hee had no prynce by her tenheryte after hym, and for alſo that ſhe was his brother's wief.

¶ *Walter's* Counſell perceavynge his entent, durſte not contrarye the ſame, hee was a man ſo headye furyous.

¶ A ſhorte and breve complaynynge againſte weake harted Counſelours, that ſhrynkethe to ſpeake in the cawſe of right, chalengeinge ſelfe wylled prynccys that will woorke (in grave mateirs) withoute ſage advyſement.

¶ A kyngis Counſell is cheiflye choaſe to ordre a kinge, and they (by feare or forſe) not to bee compelled.

¶ A kyngis Cownſell oughte to bee choaſe of thauncient ſorte, for their wiſedom and experyence, and not of younge gaddinge wittys, whoe (if they bee founde contrariqus) to have no lyttle cauſe to lament.

¶ *Walter* fully determynethe to relinquiſche *Gryſilde* his wife, for whiche, as the grave ſorte weare penſife and ſorye, the light wittys weare joyous and gladde.

¶ Of the Cardynall *Wolſaye*, whoe, counſelinge withe Aſtronomyers, founde a woman to be his undoinge, whiche (moſte wronfullye) he ymputed to goode *Griſilde*, whearfore he went into Fraunce, and labored for the Kyngis ſiſter theare, to matche withe *Walter* our Kinge.

¶ Of *Anne Bullayne*, newlye entred the Cowrte, on whom *Walter* caſte his mynde (by ſingular favour) that theare he purpoſed to ſettle hym ſelfe.

¶ A prynce his mynde onſe ſett upon a thinge (bee ytt neaver ſo wronge), flaterers abowte hym will finde cavyllations ynoughe to bringe it unto paſſe, as in this preſent caſe.

¶ They burdayne goode *Griſilde* withe ſterilenes, not conſyderinge howe all increaſe proceadethe of God.

¶ Kingis and Great men, voyde of feare of God, kepinge concubynes, He ofte cuttethe of their poſterytee, and ſuche erectethe in their places pleaſinge unto Hym.

¶ *Anne Bullayne* advaunced *Merqueſes* of *Penbrooke*, and is as Queene regarded and take, whiche ſundrye (the wiſe) muche merveyled therat, fearinge ſuche ſodayne clymbinge to have a muche ſodayne fall.

¶ *Caput* 6.

¶ Meſſengers are ſent to *Rome* for a dyvorſement, but none myght bee obteyned; *Walter* (the meane while) withe the newe Merqueſes paſſethe their tyme in huntinge and other pleaſures the Progreſſe. tyme, goode *Griſilde* (as an abjecte) attendinge upon them.

¶ The Cardynall *Wolſayes* fayle heer begynneth to avale.

¶ Twoe ſpeciall cauſes (by reporte) of the Cardynals departure oute of favour.

¶ Howe, at thende of the Progreſſe tyme, he rendred an accompte of all the treaſure that hee had, and was ſent to *Yorke*, to his See churche theare.

¶ Immedyatly, and withe greate haſte, he was ſent for backe to the Cowrte, wheare (in returnynge) he dyed at *Leceſtre* Abbaye by the way, and of his Chriſtyan and penytent ende.

¶ A note, howe, dyinge penytentlye, God of ſuche reſpectethe the ende, and not the former life.

¶ The *Authour* heereof pyteithe his deathe and departure oute of favour before the completinge his notable warke begone in *Oxforde*, wiſchinge our noble *Queene* nowe tyme and powre to fulfill his lacke.

¶ *Caput* 7.

¶ The caufe originall of the Cardynal's erectinge his College in *Oxforde*, then called *Frydifwife.*

¶ The tryfelinge of the woorekemen and lacke of goode overfeers was the vearye let of fynyfchinge the fame.

¶ The warke, to the Cardynal's vayne glory, was to-muche fumptuous, but to the glorye of God nowhit to curious.

¶ Mannys vayne pompe before Goddys glorye preferred, the warke theare can neaver take goode fucceffe.

¶ Theare fhoulde have beene readde the Seavyn lyberall Sciencies, and the cheififte learned in Chriftiandome (if theye myght have beene gote for monaye or meede) to have beene Readers in the fame.

¶ Goddis ayde was not affiftinge theare (by all toknes) bycaufe of pryde; God graunte humylytee to fulfill that pryde lacked grace to dooe.

¶ Wifchinge oure noble Queene *Marye* tyme and poure to fynyfche that yeat is lackinge in that noble fundation.

¶ The fruyte of true and perfecte learnynge, howe muche ytt furderethe to a commone utylytee.

¶ Of Doctor *Cox*, Chauncellour of *Oxforde*, a very robber, an hearetike and utter enemy to God and all goode ordre, of his robberye and dyvyllifche doingis in *Oxforde.*

¶ *Caput* 8.

¶ *Walter* revertynge his progreffe, the newe Merquefes accompayneth hym thorowe *Thame*, goode *Grifilde* commynge after, at which the goode people mut-terethe, prayinge for *Grifilde* God to preferve her.

¶ What tawlke the Commons ſecreatlye had (frynde to
frynde) upon *Walter's* exchaunginge his wife, fearynge
theareupon greate daungers to enſue.

¶ The meſſengers revert from *Rome*, unſpedde of the
thinge they traveyled for.

¶ Howe theareupon *Walter* raged and frett againſte the
Busſhoppe of *Rome*.

¶ Howe *Walter* was firſte enſenſed (by a muche light
perſon) to take upon hym the Supreamacye, whiche
by Aĉte of Perlyament (choaſen at his owne will) was
ſoone graunted.

¶ *Caput* 9.

¶ *Walter*, to appeace the worldelye rumoure, cauſed his
caſe to bee diſputed at *Oxforde*.

¶ *John Longelande* (Buſhoppe of *Lincolne*) was cheeif
Commyſſioner in the ſaide caſe.

¶ One fryer *Nicholas* (an alien) was cheeif ſoliciter for
the Kynge in this behaulfe.

¶ No indifferencye was uſed theare, for whoe that ſpake
againſte the Kingis partye weare redargued, diſdayned,
and muche cruellye threatened.

¶ And contrarye wiſe, thois leanynge to the Kinges
partye cheared, rewarded, and made of.

¶ At that buſynes theare Falſehod tryumphed, and
Truthe quaked for feare, but neaver ſhranke his hed.

¶ An *Aĉte* that ſeaſon was differred, bycauſe theiſe fyue
Inceptour Doĉtors, *Mawdelaye, Mooreman, Holyman,
Mortymer,* and *Cooke,* wolde (in nowiſe) agree to the
dyvorſement, whiche fyue weare notable clarkes all.

¶ The *Acte*, at the lafte, tooke place by treatye the
Proctors made to Bufshope *Langelande* for their
owne fpecial availe.

¶ On *Lincoln's* College gate, wheare Bufshoppe *Longelande* laye, weare gallowes made withe chalke, and
ropyffe of hempe fafte nayled thearby, fignyfyinge
that hee and hys weare worthie the lyke for their
goinge againfte the truthe.

¶ Goode women in *Oxforde* couraged the mateir fore
on goode *Grifildis* partye, and had foyled fryer *Nicholas*
and other of that forte, if ther handys myght have
ferved to their harts.

¶ Howe, thorowe fryer *Nicholas* complaynte, á thirty
women (or neare theareaboutys) weare empryfoned in
Buckerdo for thre dayes fpace and three nyghtys.

¶ Howe the Regeaunte Maifters (at that tyme) wolde
by nomeanys graunte the Unyverfiteis feale to thagre-
ment of *Gryfildis* dyvorfinge.

¶ A Convocatio of certayne called by Bufshoppe *Long-
lande* (after longe tarryinge in vayne), whear they ftale
the Unyverfyteeis feale to fuche falfe inftrment [*fic*]
as thei had contrived.

¶ What forowe and lamentation (withe tearys) was made
of manye goode Graduates and Studentes for ftealynge
the Unyverfyteeis feale.

¶ Howe tenne to one of the Unyverfytie of *Oxforde*
ftucke to the verytee on goode *Grifildis* partye, if they
myght have beene hearde.

¶ What calamyteis and myferyes enfued in this Royalme
upon the goinge furthe of this dyvorfement, and fpe-
cyally upon ufurpinge the Supreamacye.

¶ Upon this occaſion downe went *Croſſes, Churcheſſe, Abbayes, Collegies, Chauntries, Hoſpitales,* and ſundrye put to deathe moſte unmerſyfullye.

¶ *Caput* 10.

¶ *Walter* preſented withe the Unyverſyteeis ſeale, he made nowe no ſtoppe, but furdered his purpoſe, hee had no maner á lett.

¶ *Walter* ſendethe to *Griſilde* to rendre up her Crowne, whiche ſhee (utterlye) denyeth to dooe, withe ſuche wittye and reaſonable anſweare that *Walter* was moſte ſore offended thearewitheall.

¶ *Griſilde* is heere avoyded the Cowrte to wheare as *Walter* pleaſethe to aſſigne her.

¶ The greateſt greeif to goode *Griſildis* hart was that ſhe myght have no comforte of her Dowghters companye, whoe laye then at *Ludlowe* and was kept from her of ſett purpoſe.

¶ The Dowghter, heearinge her mothers uncharytable entreatinge, moſte pytefullye lamentethe her caſe.

¶ Of *Walter's* great ſolicitude in this mateir, who wolde bee ſeene to dooe all uprightlye, and his feche was cleane to the contraye.

¶ *Caput* 11.

¶ A Cowrte *Walter* aſſignethe at *Dunſtable,* wheare goode *Griſilde* was depryved her regale eſtate, and theare was geaven to name the ladye *Douagere.*

¶ What daungre enſuethe to breache of faithe when pryncis dooe ſtrey from their bownden promyſes.

¶ For breache of faithe and promyfes made, this Royalme hathe beene plaged, and yeat (at this daye) is not all free.

¶ *Caput* 12.

¶ *Gryfilde* (after her depofition) was fent to *Bugden* (to a freendys place of hers) theare to fojourne.

¶ What goodnes goode *Gryfilde* fownde at that frindis handys, *John Longelande*, Buffoppe of *Lincolne*.

¶ Theare at *Bugden* all her olde offycers weare commaunded from her, and newe put in their places, to the great admynyftringe of forowes to her harte.

¶ Of her lamentabl takinge her leave of her olde mofte truftye and lovynge fervauntys.

¶ Howe grevouflye *Grefilde* tooke it that fhe myght not fo amplye departe to the pooare as fhe was wonte to dooe ; She refufethe all mundayne comfortinge, and betaketh her whoale to the merciful difpofition of Almyghty God.

¶ Of her often complaynynge unto her felfe of *Walters* unkindenes unto her, and fhe fo lovynge unto hym. Howe fhe (fpecially) endeavored, for all her trobles, to avoyde murmuration.

¶ Of her malignours fhe wifchethe amendement of life, and not that God fholde oughtis revenge her cawfe.

¶ She neaver wolde curffe or blame her mysfortune or myfentreatinge, lamentinge muche rather others daungers enfuynge then her owne.

¶ *Caput* 13.

¶ *Gryfilde* removed to *Conmolton* in Huntyngedone-

D

ſheere; God theare viſitinge her withe ſikenes, perceavynge her tyme come to departe this life, moſte chriſtyanlye ſhe prepared thearfore.

¶ She beſought no bodelye phiſike, but to be diſſolved, that her ſpirite myght bee with Chriſte.

¶ What moſte Chriſtian waies ſhee tooke for her ſauſe walkinge oute of this myſerable life, to bee adnoted of eache goode Chriſtian (when tyme ſhall come) to practice the like.

¶ *Firſte*, ſhe became moſte penytent in harte for what-ſoeaver offenſe towardys God or the worlde ſhe had commytted.

¶ *Next*, ſhe ſore lamented that eaver ſhe ſet delectation of mynde upon worldely thinge before her Lorde God.

¶ *Thyrdele*, withe meeke contrition and harte fixed upon the Paſſion of Chriſte, ſhe evermore cryed to Hym for mercye.

¶ *Fowrthelye*, ſhe conſydered that whoeſo deſyrethe of God forgevenes of ſynnes ought firſte to dooe the ſame to other, wheafore (*ſic*) ſhe forgeavethe all the worlde as ſhee wolde bee forgeaven of God.

¶ *Then*, takinge her Goſtelye Father, her whoale lyfe (diſpleaſinge unto God) moſte penytentlye to hym ſhe declarethe.

¶ *Fynallye*, receavynge the *Euchariſte* moſte reverentlye, ſhe thought her ſelfe in goode waye againſte her utter howre ſholde come.

¶ She takethe her leave of this worlde in muche Chriſtian ſorte, of *Walter* (with muche openynge her mynde unto hym, partelye for her buryall, partylye for her Dowghter *Marye*) of her *Freendys*, her *Foes*, her

Servauntys, of *Lordys*, *Ladyes*, *Knyghtys*, *Gentlemen*, and *Commoners*.

¶ *Caput* 14.

¶ Heere goode *Gryſilde* (muche motherlye) takethe her leave of her Dowghter *Marye*, commendinge her unto Goddys mercye and bleſſed tuytion, withe muche motherlye and godlye admonytions, bleſſinge her withe the bleſſinge that the holye Fathers *Abraham*, *Iſahac* and *Jacob* bleſſed their children.

¶ *Caput* 15.

¶ The daye preſent of *Gryſildis* departinge oute of this life, munyted (as is ſaide) withe the Sacramentys of the Churche and nowe alſo withe the *Extreme Unction*, ſhee rendrethe her ſowle to God eaverlaſtynge.

¶ So weare her trobles heere brought to an ende, and muche alteringys (concernynge her cawſe) ceaſſed, but newe (far warſſe) began, that ceaſſed not of longe tyme after.

¶ Somuche the Authour heereof confeſſethe he hathe not of this goode woman heere made mentyon as other (yeat lyvynge) better inſtructed in her holye life can dooe

¶ *Caput* 16.

¶ Howe *Walter* willethe the bodye of *Gryſilde*, accordinge to her nobilitee, in *Peterburrowe* churche to be entiered much honorablye.

¶ The maner (fome parte) of the conveyaunce of the faide bodye (withe offycers and mynyfters) to wheare it fholde refte, muche parte expreffinge of the funerall obfequye.

¶ Of whois feparation oute of this life all goode folke joyed, bycaufe fhe, lyvynge well, cowlde not after-wardys myfcary.

¶ Whoefo lyvethe at luftes lybertee after vitious forte, his ende is to bee dowbted, thearfore befte is in tyme to ufe vertue, for the deathe of the Goode in the fight of God is preacious.

¶ The portion or rewarde ordayned for the Evyll is Fyer and Sulphur everlaftingelye deputed for them to boyle yn.

¶ *Gryfilde* for her heere abhorringe of fynne and piteinge the pooare hathe nowe in heavyn everlaftinge rewarde.

¶ God fo provyded that thoughe *Grifilde* was heere depryved her Crowne, He rendred her another that eaver fhall endure.

¶ *Caput* 17.

¶ The cheeif mooarner in the funerals of this goode *Gryfildis* exequye was her mofte tendre and lovynge Doughter *Marye*, to whome (in comparafon for that behaulfe) all the other mooarners weare but countrefettes as in her lamentation for her faide mother and com-mendation of her to God dothe plentyouflye appeare.

¶ *Caput* 18.

¶ A conferrynge betweene the *Firfte Grifilde* and the

Seconde, the *Firſte Walter* and the *Seconde*, fomuche provynge the *Seconde Gryſilde* of more authorytee as ſhe was a *Chriſtian*, the other an *Ethnyke*, ſhe a noble woman of byrthe and delycatlye brought upp, thearfore the more harder adverſytee tendure, thother farre baſe[r] brought upp in penurye and hardenes, brought to the fame ſtate agayne ſhe myght the eafyer ſuffre ytt.

¶ Somuche as is betweene *earneſt* and *game*, fo was the unkyndenes doone to this *Seconde Griſilde* of more ymportaunce then to the *Firſte*, for ſhe, relinquyſched, was receaved agayne, fo did her *Walter* but dyſſemble withe her. But this *Seconde Gryſilde*, depoſed of her honour, was neaver thearto receaved agayne, fo was ſhe cruellye uſed and dallyed witheall.

¶ The *Firſte Walter* his children tendered moſte honorably, *thother Walter* abacinge his ſeade much unnaturally.

¶ *Walter* the *Firſte* ignoraunte of Goddys lawe, bycawſe he was an Inſydele, fomuche his offence the leſſe if he had played the like parte; but *Walter* the *Seconde* a Chryſtyan, fomuche a greate deale his fawte the greater.

¶ This comparaſon, *Walter withe Walter* and *Griſilde withe Gryſilde*, maye well ferve for *Title* of this hiſtorye.

¶ Howe muche this Hiſtorye of the *Seconde Gryſilde* is withe manye (at this preſent daye) knowne to be true, the other doubtefull and to bee but fayned ſuppoſed of manye, fomuche then maye this bee take in more authorytee.

¶ Sithe *Ethnykes* (of olde) their famous women put in

recòrdys to their poſterytee, howe muche ought wee *Chriſtyans* then, and muche more, to dooe the ſame.
¶ Thautor of this, wrytinge the ſame partely by know-ledge and paretelye by heearinge ſaye, if (thearfore) oughtys bee heere ſownde contraryinge the Truthe, he humblye ſubmyttethe it to the reformation of other.
¶ A ſpeciall and moſte probable tryall *Gryſildys* maryage to bee moſte lawfull and goode.
¶ Howe heavyn and earthe (ſpecially the goode ſorte) rejoyced in the exaltynge of *Gryſildys* ſeade to the hie eſtate.

¶ *Caput* 19.

¶ *Gryſilde*, joyinge the heavynly felycitee (as wee fully truſte), dothe praye for us theare is no myſdoubtys.
¶ A probation howe Saynctes (by God) dothe knowe oure thoughtes and alſo (of charytee) dothe praye for us.
¶ A contemplation of this Author, after what ſorte (may bee thought) the heavynly Courte dothe praye for ſynners, as for oure Englande late owte of the waye.

¶ *Caput* 20.

¶ Heere concludeth the Author howe in *Gryſilde* nobilytee and meekenes weare mett, thoughe ſeelden ſo ſeene in one Eſtate mundayne.
¶ Howe (of meekenes) ſhe inclyned herſelfe lowe, thynkynge of thearthe to yſſue and thearin agayne to be reſolved.
¶ Of meekenes ſhe vyſited the pooare, ſhe daylye was

kneelynge in prayer, at myddenyght geavynge her felfe to contemplation, fufferynge adverfite without murmuration.

¶ Wrongefull entreatinge, fightynge agaynfte the Dyvyll, the Worlde and the Flefche, fufferinge for Right-uoufnes fake, maye well bee called a Martyrdome.

¶ *Heere endethe the Table.*

¶ *An* Oration confolatory *to our mofte dreade foveraigne Queene* Marye *to comforte her felfe in God, by example of* Jofeph, *funne unto* Jacob *the holye Patriarke; whome, after his great trobles, God fet in honor and florifchinge eftate above all the pryncis of the worlde, as Hee hathe her above all ladyes and women.*

[This "Oration" is appended by the Author at the end of his book.]

¶ *Heere enſuethe a true and moſte notable Hiſtorye of a* [ſ. 11.]
right noble and famous ladye produced in Spayne, in-
tytuled, THE SECONDE GRISILDE, praɛticed
not longe oute of this tyme, in muche parte tragedous,
as deleɛtable bothe to Heearers and Readers.

¶ *Caput Primum.*

 RYTERS hathe manye endeauored their   *Twoe cauſes*
   paynes   *why wryters*
               endeaver their
   Hiſtoryes famous to put in recordis, *paynes.*
   Some for their praɛtice, ſome for meede
      or gaynes,
   Muche delytinge bothe to ladyes and
      lordis,
In whiche their ſtiles and pryncipall exordis
Muche ornatlye, as ſeemed to them beſte,
They ſawe the ſame moſte floriſcheingely dreſte.

Whois worthie ſteppis enſuynge (as I can) *The goode*
(Thoughe an ydiot the probate ſapyentis) *Queene*
I heere entende of á noble woman   *Catharyne.*
(As addinge of myne to their preaſydentys)
To wright and ſet furthe the godly talentis,
For an exampler in ſome maner ſute,
Oother of vertue to take thearby frute.

E

Her meekenes ſpeciallye ſurmountynge.

Whoe, for her paſſinge noble vertues,
Specially meekenes in aduerſytee,
In all hiſtoryes of Gentyls or Jues,
As vnfaynedly ſeemethe vnto mee,
To her maye no juſte comparaſon bee ;
Wronged as ſhee was, meekely to ſuſtayne
Almoſte it was a thinge farre inhumayne.

This noble woman Catharyne, *for her meeknes, applied to* Gryſilde.
[f. 11b.]

This noble ladye, this godlye *Gryſilde*,
So applied for onlye the propretee,
On whome we purpoſe oure mateir to bilde,
As to entreat by goode authorytee,
As probate witneſſies hathe learned mee,
Concernynge her Countrey, to name ſpeciall,
In *Spayne* ſhee had her firſte oryginall.

Her Fathers name Ferdynande, *her mother called* Elizabeth.

Doughter ſhee was to one *Ferdynande*,
Kynge of *Spayne* and *Cicilye* alſo ;
Her mother was called, as I vndreſtande,
Elizabethe, as oother ſundrye mo ;
After, when firſte ſhee was hable to go,
To nuriſche her in ſorte to her degree,
Ladyes weare choaſe, the beſte that gote myght bee.

Howe ſhe had aptenes to all vertuous exercyſes.

In literate knowledge entred ſhee was,
By lyttle and lyttle, as ſhee in age grwe,
Towardiſlye althingis withe her came to paſſe
That ſpecially framed vnto vertue ;
Suche inſtincte of grace God can her indue,
That by her vertues in ſo tendre age
Shee ſhoulde of honour aſcende the worthie ſtage.

Afcendinge vpp to more maturytee,
Attaynynge to perfecte difcretion
Alwayes an inclynation had fhee
To lowlynes, that cheeif perfection,
Gatheringe, as rule for her direction,
In holye Scriptures howe theare is alowde
All meekenes of God, refiftinge the prowde.

Deus fuberbis
(fic) refiftit,
humilibus dat
gratiam.
[1 Pet. v. 5.]

Of her perfonage defcription to make,
She was right comely and chearful withe all;
In voyce, fomewhat bigge fowndinge fhe fpake;
In ftature, but meane, and bonarly withe all;
Her coolour fanguyne, that men dothe befte call;
What to this purpofe neadethe more to bee tolde?
She was a ladye pleafaunte to beeholde.

*Of her forme
and perfon-
age.*
[f. 12.]

So perfecte fhe was not in perfonage,
But farre perfecter was her inwarde mynde;
To voyde all wilful infolent outerage
(Exited by carnal voluptee blynde)
This remeadye (by grace) fhe wolde befte fynde,
To geeve herfelfe to contemplation
In whiche was muche her exercitation.

Pulchra facie,
fed pulchrior
mente.

Greatlye fhe loued to heeare and to reade
The holye Scriptures mofte fpeciallye,
Alfo the lyues of Sainctys that bee deade,
To holye life that muche myght edifie;
In whiche accuftomynge cuftomablie,
It was a certaigne fpiritual habyte
That clofed her from this worldis vayne delyte.

*Howe fhe
favored the
Scriptures of
God and the
lyues of
Sainctes.*

Howe ſhe not delyted in vayne toyes, but alwayes in vertuous buſyneſſes.

Withe ſtoole and needyl ſhe was not to ſeeke
And oother praċtycingis for ladyes meete ;
To paſtyme at Tables, Ticktacke or Gleeke,
Cardys, Dyce, or vayne toyes accuſtomed yeete,
She thought not ſeemed for women diſcreete,
But weare incitamentys to ſinne and vice,
Whearfore ſhe gaue her to oother exercife.

Of her exercife bothe moarn-ynge and nyght on her kneeis in prayer.

[*f.* 12ᵇ.]

Every moarnynge and alſo at nyght
Twoe howres (at the leaſte) on kneeis wolde ſhe ſitte,
Commendinge herſelfe to God moſte of myght,
Her life that Hee wolde alwayes ordre itt,
From ſynne by His grace as to prohybit,
That to His will moſte honorable
Herſe myght bee euermore conformable.

To pooare as riche ſhe was chearfull, to all goode deadys alwaies ready to doo her ſur-theraunce

To euery creature, riche other poore,
Shee ſhewed herſelfe moſte amyably,
Of contention ſhe loued no ſtoore,
But to bee in quyet ſpecially ;
Her life ſhee heere ledde muche charitably,
To what goode deade that anyman woulde
Readye alwaies to dooe the beſte ſhee coulde.

She was pyte-ful and ful of mercye vnto the pooare.

As ſhe was chearful to creatures all,
So was ſhe euermore muche pitefull ;
Her charitee to the pooare was not ſmall,
To dooe them comforte ſhe wolde not bee dull,
No vertuous deade ſhe wolde diſanull
But muche rather the vttermuſte ſhe myght,
Wheare ſlacknes was, the partyes to exite.

But for fhe was her parentys yeat vndre,
So amplye fhe coulde not her mynde extende,
Yeat at her dooingis dyverfe dyd wundre,
And in their hartys did her greatly commende ;
Whateauer fhe did was to a goode ende,
Only (as to faye) Goddis fpecyal praife,
Vayne glory (as Deathe) deteftinge alwaife.

*Her deadys
orderynge to
Goddys fpecial
praife, and not
to anye vayne
glorye.*

The youthe that to her weare affociat,
As vpon her, their miftreffe, to attende,
Vfinge taches light and illicitat,
She thearof wolde them mofte ftreitely defende,
Withe oother meanys if thei lifte not amende,
So that in that parte (whiche was meruelous)
Her Courte was as it had been Religious.

*Howe her
Cowrte was
as Religious,
for bryngynge
vpp of her
yowthe.
[f. 13.]*

For princelye behauyour, nurture, and fuche
To womanlynes that did appertayne,
None myght (certaynely) commende her to muche,
She had in that kinde the vearye right veyne ;
Of her princelye prefence all men weare fayne,
Not onlye the cheif had fuche affection
But alfo the pooare had her in dilection.

*For her prynce-
ly behauyoure,
bathe poore and
riche defyred
her prefence.*

She was a woman of wondreful grace
As in oure age of long tyme did fpringe,
All vertue fpecially fhe did embrace
And vice (of truthe) vtterly contempnynge,
Whiche was wondreful in fo younge a thinge ;
But, wheare God geavethe illumynation,
Mufte neadys fhewe light of goode conuerfation,

*Wheare God
infpirethe to
grace, mufte
neadys profper
vnto the fame.*

As ſhe was vertuous inwardelye, ſo ſhe ordred her outwardys example.

To whiche ſhe had a ſpecyall reſpecte,
Afwel her outwardys whoale faſhyonynge
By euyl example on none to reflecte,
As inwardelye ſhe abhorred ſuche thinge,
Muche prudently this wiſe conſyderinge,
Whois example inducethe to lightnes
Obumbrethe of Grace the gloſſinge brightnes.

[ſ. 13ᵇ.] ¶ *Howe this noble* Seconde Gryſilde *was marryed into*
Greate Brytayne, *to a moſte worthie and towardys Prynce*
theare, called Arthur, *whoe lyued withe her but uery ſhorte*
tyme, ſo (in his tendre age) departinge this life, and of
her piteful lamentation for hym.

¶ *Caput* 2.

The brute of this ladye blowne (by reporte) into Englande.

HIS princely lady, *Griſilde*, (as wee name,)
Withe her deere parentes abidinge in *Spaine*,
Whois paſſinge worthynes was blowne by fame
Vnto the noble cowntrey of *Brytayne*,
Wheare at that tyme a famous kynge did reigne,
Oute of this life departed longe agone,

Henrye the Seavynthe.

Called (in his tyme) the *Seconde Salomon*.

Of Prynce Arthur, *and of his pryncely towardnes.*

Unto this kinge of famous memorye
A prynce theare was, moſte goodly floriſchinge,
By name *Arthur*, ſo called proprelye,
In all this worlde no towarder younge thinge;
Whois famous Father that tyme thus caſtinge
That as he was noble in eſtate
To haue hym machte accordinge to the rate.

This prudent kinge in *Spayne* that tyme herde tell
To bee this ladye, fayre *Gryſilidis*,
Withe pryncely vertues howe ſhe did excell,
That towardys her his mynde occupied is,
Counſelinge thearin withe Counſelours of his,
Whiche debated throughe ſage aduiſement
Founde it to bee thinge moſte expedient.

*Counſell tak-
inge for the
maryage of this
ladye* Catha-
ryne.

After, with ſpeede, ambaſſadours weare ſent
Vpon this marryage for to entreat,
Which, on that one partye wayed to entent,
And on the other by polecye greate,
For to conclude their braynes they much did beate,
As for bothe partyes ſeeamed to the beſte
That myght be cauſe of tranquillytee and reſte.

*Meſſengers ſent
for entreatye
of the ſayde
marryage.*
[f. 14.]

This weyghtye mateir brought to concluſion,
Our *Britayne* ambaſſadours whome did reverte,
In whiche was wrought no maner colluſion,
But faitheful true meanynge on either parte;
To whiche goode *Griſilde* graunted her whoale harte,
And ſhortely after, moſt worthelye, as ſhe ought,
Into *Brytayne* was honorablye brought,

*The marryage
concluded be-
tweene Prynce
Arthur and
the Ladye
Catharyne.*

Wheare the deſpouſaile was ſolemplye kepte,
Withe ſuche worthie tryumphe as did belonge;
But the marryed togeathers not ſlepte,
For the ſaide Prynce was but tendre and yonge,
Leſte to his growinge it myght dooe muche wronge;
Yeat, notwitheſtandinge that myght not bee had,
Either of oother weare paſſingelye glad.

*The deſpouſaile
ſolemply kept
witheoute car-
nall cognytion.*

*Prynce Ar-
thur, withyn
ſhorte ſpace
after his mar-
ryage, depar-
ted this life.*

But, well awaye! halas the heauye caſe!
After this myrthe and ioyous felycitee,
Togeathers in healthe they ioyed no longe ſpace,
This noble Prynce this life departed hee,
For whome was ſorowinge of euery degree,
Moſte ſpecially of faire *Gryſilidis*,
So ſoone her deeareſte in ſuche wiſe to myſſe.

*The doleful
lamentation of
this younge lady
for her looue
late departed.
[f. 14ᵇ.]*

"Halas" (ſhe ſaide) " what happe is me betyde
My ſpeciall jewell aboue oother all
Thus to forgoe, no lengre to abyde,
To my great greeif and hynderaunce not ſmall!
O Lorde of heauyn! which pleaſidſte hym to call
Vnto Thy heauynly celeſtiall preſence,
Bee Thou my ayde, my ſuccour, and defenſe!

*The cruelnes of
Deathe whoe
vſethe all men
alyke.*

"Thou wotiſte I am come oute of farre countraye
Heere hoapinge (throughe Thee) in ioye to haue dwelte,
But nowe, ſithe withe me it hapnethe this waye,
No lyttle care is of me to bee felte.
O Deathe! whie haſte thou thus cruelly delte?
I dare not on thee make exclamation,
For me thou wilte vſe after like faſhion.

*She deſirethe
(if God ſo
wolde) to bee
ſeperat oute of
this life.*

"Evyn nowe, O Lorde, if it myght ſo pleaſe Thee,
Then ſhoulde I no more of worldely greeif taiſte;
To bee withe my *Arthur* beſte weare for mee,
Withe hym of Thie joyes to haue like repaiſte.
If (to Thie pleaſure) my woordis bee in waiſte,
(For that throughe ſorowe my wittis are wexte groſe)
Bee it (O Lorde) as Thou liſte to diſpoſe.

" And, merciful God, Kinge of Kyngys all,
Woorke Thou for me nowe mofte mercifullye ;
Sithe hither Thou pleafidfte me thus to call,
Geue me not vpp to lyue myferablye,
But, as I purpofe to ferve Thee trulye,
So fauorablye for mee Thou prouyde,
And in my neade to bee alwaies my Guyde.

Of God fhe befeachethe fpeciall ayde, as fhe myndeth to ferve Hym.

" Thee haue I ay fownde to this prefent daye
My fpecial goode Lorde and faufe Protećtor ;·
As Thou hafte fo beene, fo bee thou alwaye
To me a gratious fryndlye Refpećtor
And withe Thie Grace a daylye Refećtor,
That this or oother the like tribulation
From Thee of mee make no feparation.

*She alwayes tooke God her fpecyall Protećtor.
[f. 15.]*

" In hither repayringe to forefaide entent
My frindis to this ende had expećtation
I to haue profperde wheare deathe can preuent,
And they to haue ioyed in oure generation,
Whiche all is nowe brought to defolation,
After this fayinge, ' Thoughe man proponethe,
God as Hee pleafethe althingis difpofethe.'

Howe God difpofethe, howe eauer man proponethe.

" Hoapinge fuche wife in my profperous fucceffe
Withe me they departed verye largelye ;
Vpon this myfhappe what maye they nowe geffe
But me to accompte for mofte vnhappye ?
Theis all to my harte breedethe no fmall coarfye,
Takinge as worthelye fent vnto mee
For my former life and inyquytee.

She takethe this greeif for her demerytes.

F

Howe God can ordayne is not for man to ſearche.
" I take it of Goddys prouyſion ſent
As I not worthie withe hym to remayne,
Or for ſome oother farre ſecrete entent
Whiche Hee alone in Hymſelfe dothe conteyne,
Whois counſellis occulte howe He can ordayne
Surmountethe mannys inueſtigation,
So myghtie is His domynation.

Why hym or her God tak- ethe is not for man to deſyne.
[*ſ.* 15ᵇ.]
" Whie Hee tooke hym and mee heere lefte behynde,
Or whie not mee and hym to let ſurvyue,
I cannot termyne in perfecte true kynde,
I cannot the cauſe compaſſe or contryue ;
Hee ordaynethe for bothe the deadde and the lyue
All to the beſte ; wee ought no leſſe to ſaye,
Oure willys to His will willyngely tobeye.

This worlde ofte workethe contraryouſlye for our vn- godlynes.
" Sithe ſo behovethe (thoughe Nature fraylelye
Ympugnethe by muche contraryetee),
Praye will I for hym, beſte is ſo, daylye,
And take (as God ſendthe) this worldys varyetee,
Whiche ſhewthe contrarious for oure ympyetee,
For doubteles thorowe oure ſynnes occaſion
Ofte hapnethe on vs Goddys indignation.

Regum 2°, 12 *capite.*
" Sometyme for Father Hee plagethe the Chylde,
As *Davyths* childe yſſued of *Berſabe* ;
Sometyme the Father for Chyldren wylde
Regum *primo*, 1111 *capite.*
As *Hely* ; whoe liſte the *Regums* goe ſee ;
Sometyme for the owne propre inyquytee,
But not ſo of my Love I dare well ſaye,
For plyant hee was to vertue alwaye.

"Thoughe for his owne fawte, fathers, or mothers,
He was not henſe take I thynke in my harte,
It myght (perhaps) bee, as Scripture dothe reherſe,
Leſte the Malignour his ſenſys myght peruerte
To what God wolde to become overthwarte,
Or, as Eſay ſayinge in this wiſe,
Hee was henſe take from this worldys malice.

Raptus eſt ne malitia mutaret intelleƈtum illius. *Sapi.* 4. [11.]

C[ap] 53.

" This wayes or that wayes, this is moſte certayne,
God (at His pleaſure) hathe ſent for hym henſe;
To contrarye Hym it weare but in vayne,
I yeealde me as pleaſethe His magnyficenſe,
Hym beſeachinge to take me to His preſence,
That as in cleannes we weare heere vnyte
So to taſſotiat in His heauynlye ſight.

To contrarye Goddys ordynaunce weare but in vayne. [f. 16.]

" For, I adnotinge this worldys behauyour,
All is in the ſame but playne vanytee,
Rather pluckynge from Chriſte (my Sauyoure)
Then to His pleaſure applyaunte to bee;
Whearfore I feele it beſte ſhall behoue mee
From worldely vanyteis mee to withedrawe,
And to endeauer Goddys looue and dwe awe.

All in this worlde of worldly mynyſtrynge is but vanytee.

" I ſee heere troble and muche vexation,
I ſee heere the higheſt hathe none aſſuraunce,
I ſee and feele heere muche temptation,
I ſee no man hathe heere contynuaunce;
This worlde conſyderinge of ſuche inconſtaunce
Whoe is but will take it accordinglye?
As, God! (I beſeache) ſo alwayes maye I!

This worlde is of none aſſuraunce but ful of myſery.

Of Gryſilde

Heere is the tyme of pere-grynation to-wardys the worlde to come.
" So to vſe this vayne worldelye eſtate
As but oure tyme of peregrynation;
So caſtinge for the joyes intermynat
Withe all hartys earneſte inclynation,
Meekely ſufferinge heere trybulation
(Whatſoeauer God ſhall pleaſe to ordayne),
The heauynlye fruition for to attayne."

Reaſon will-ethe to bee con-tented as God ordaynethe.
[f. 16ᵇ.]
Suche was this maydyns meditation
After her Loues departure this life,
Settinge aſyde all conſolation,
Reaſon and *Frayletie* within her at ſtrife ;
Reaſon wylled her, thoughe late ſhe weare wife
To bee contented as God liſte to ſende,
Thoughe (inwardelye) *Frayltie* muche did contende.

For longe tyme after her ſor-owes endured for her Looue.
But, for all that, the lamentation
(Longe tyme enduringe) of this noble mayde,
After her Loues ſo expiration,
It cannot of mee bee thorowlye ſayde ;
All ſumptuous attyrementes weare aſide layde,
Her chriſtall iyen for longe tyme after
Weare as a lymbecke diſtillinge cleare water.

Great weare the ſorowes bothe of Father and Mother and all the Royalme for the ſaide Prince.
The heavye cheare bothe of Father and Mother
And of the whoale Royalme to longe weare to tell,
But, for myne entent is this and none other
Cheiflye tentreat of this noble Damoyſell,
The reſte (for this ſeaſon) I wyll let dwell,
And ferdre wright howe, after heauynes,
Her joyes agayne began for to encreſe.

¶ *Heere* Gryſilde *is marryed to* Walter (*her firſte huſ-bondys brother*); *his Father dyethe, and* Walter *withe* Gryſilde *crowned Kynge and Ꝗyeene, beetweene whome theare ſpryngethe a Prynce whoe lyuethe but ſmall tyme, and afterwardys a Princeſſe called* Marye, *and of Goddis wondrefull workeynge for her.*

¶ *Caput* 3.

HIS towardys younge Prince departed and gone [ſ. 17.]
And his funeral obſequye cleane paſte,
His famous Father, the *Seconde Salomon,*
(Wyttelye thus weyinge) began at the laſte
In his inwarde mynde to compaſſe and caſte
For this noble ladye howe to ordayne
That ſo was hither yſſued from *Spayne.*

At the concludinge of the mateir furſte
It was agreed, if the Prynce dyd departe
A *Douarye* (of duetye) neadys have ſhe muſte;
Whiche nowe the kynge reuoluethe in his harte,
Conſyderinge he maye not from his promyſſe ſtarte.
Pryncys in their leaugis to bee fownde doble,
Is cawſe (oftetymes) of muche hate and troble.

Ferdre, as thus confyderinge alſo
This ſaide noble ladye whome to repayre,
And yeearely ſuche *Douarye* from henſe to goe
By her exchaungeinge this ſoyle or layre,
Yeat rather he caſte (ſyttinge in his chayre)
So that it myght bee conuenyently doone,
To haue her marrye withe his oother ſoone.

For at that ſeaſon, beſydis thother deadde,
He had a ſoone whiche *Walter* had to name,
That nowe was Prynce heere in his brothers ſteadde,
For whome his Father dothe buſelye frame,
As ſaide is before, taccompliſche the ſame,
In whiche he dyd moſte wyttye counſell take
That wyttelye cowlde for the purpoſe make.

[ſ. 17ᵇ.] Bycauſe the caſe was ſeelden ſeene in vre
One brother to marrye withe the other's wife,
To dooe that their dooingis myght take effecte ſure
Afterwardys to bee deuoyde of all ſtrife,
Withe diligent ſearche, throughe meanys exceſſyue,
All Chriſtian clergye they did examyne
Vpon the ſaide caſe, what they cowlde defyne.

Whiche (certaynly) not headely and ſoone
But withe muche ſobre deliberation,
Fownde (by goode learnynge) it myght well bee doone,
So defynynge in their Conuocation ;
After, yeat ferdre, for more confyrmation,
This ſage *Salomon*, to voyde all maner blame,
Sent vnto *Rome* to haue judged the ſame.

Wheare then the *Buſſhoppe* withe his whoale Counſell,
Examynynge (trulye) the foreſaide caſe,
As thynge probable, lawful and well,
They it ſo tryed in conuenyent ſpace
Confirmynge the ſame, remyttinge apace
The meſſengers ſo in the mateir ſent,
Their Kynge to proceeade in his goode entent.

Vpon whiche notable approbation
This noble ladye was marryed agayne
To the faide *Walter*, of highe commendation
For his perfonage, fo paffinge foueraigne,
Whoe (certaynlye), as I beleue certayne,
For comelynes and ftature to accownte
No Prynce (then lyuynge) theare dyd hym furmowte (*fic*).

Ere longe tyme after, this faide *Salomon*   [*f.* 18.]
By God was fent for to an other life ;
Walter (his fpon) the Crowne tooke hym vpon,
Crownynge alfo Queene goode *Grifilde* his wife,
Betweene whiche twoe flowres, to ceaffe heere all ftrife,
A Prynce theare fprang mofte beawtious to fee
And to name *Arthur* (certaynlye) had hee.

Of whome this whoale Royalme was paffingely glad,
·· Mofte highely hoaping in his pofterytee ;
But, after fhorte fpace, hee made them all fad
For, of his life heere the fhorte breuytee,
Henfe was hee take by Deathes crudelytee,
Throughe what occafion I cannot defyne
But that it pleafed God fo to affigne.

Thoughe *Walter* (the Father) manfully and ftowte,
(Muche ftryuynge againfte Nature ynwardelye)
Afmuche as hee myght, beare the mateir owte,
Yeat to his harte (nodoutes) it went ful nye ;
But, tochinge the Mother fpecyallye,
Neauer was theare woman (I thinke noleffe)
That for her childe myght fhewe more heauynes.

Shee wepte, ſhee ſuobbed, ſhee ſighed ofte witheall,
Shee wrounge her handys of motherly pytee,
‿Shee wolde not holde ſtate vndre cloth of pall,
Shee whoale forgote her highe regalytee
Shee tooke his deathe as moſte calamytee,
For that it was her firſte begoten childe,
For whome all joyes ſhe vtterlye exilde.

[ƒ. 18ᵇ.]

Nother wolde ſhee in companye frequent,
Nother wolde ſhee in pleaſures oughtes delyte,
Nother wolde ſhee harken to inſtrument,
Nother yeat paſſe what tawlke men did recyte,
Nother wolde ſhee her feeadinge appetyte ;
Rather ſhee wolde, then oughtes of theis enure,
Shewe cheeare as ſymple or baſched creature.

This wiſe ſhee wolde her ſelfe ofte tymes complayne,
" My louelye childe (halaſſe !) I haue forlorne
Whome into this life I yealded with payne,
Thoughe to my comforte, when hee was heere borne,
And nowe ſo ſooane his life to bee oute worne
That was ſomuche my conſolation ;
No merueyle then of my lamentation.

" Hee was my worldely cheif ioye and comforte,
Nexte to my lorde and ſoueraigne huſbande,
For hym I ſure had muche vauntinge reporte
Of highe and eke meane thorowe all this lande ;
The cauſe, ſo cauſinge, no lengre to ſtande
I haue nowe loſte, omyttinge my ſweete ſoone,
The joye, the looue, that earſte I had ſo woone.

" I haue omytted that longe I dyd defire,
A Prynce, this Royalme in quyet ftate in ftaye ;
Howe maye I (agayne) another requyre ?
To tempte my Lorde God I feare, and fo maye.
A Deathe ! why hafte thoue hym taken awaye,
So highe á treafure as (lyuynge) was hee,
And fo to thoufandys afwell as to mee.

" Hee was not as chylde of the commone forte,   [*f.* 19.]
Hee was a Prynce and heyre vnto á Kinge,
Somuche the heauyer his tyme heere fo fhorte,
Somuche the more myfte for State contynuynge,
Somuche the more for hym my forowynge,
Somuche for hym my contynuall mone ;
I was á mother, and nowe am none."

Longe bode this lady and excellent Prynceffe
Lamentynge her chyldis this life departure,
Longe laye in her harte by muche heauynes
The thynge whiche in no wife fhe myght agayne recure,
Nature compelled her fo to endure,
For, as fhe was benynge in her eftate,
So was fhe (by nature) affeétionat.

Affeétionat fhe was vnto all vertue,
Thoughe not affeétionat to her felfe will ;
Affeétionat fhe was peace to contynue,
For that caufe her loue laye her childe fo vntill ;
Her will was hee fhoulde the State heere fulfill
When *Walters* breathe oute of this life did yeeade,
But otherwife God had thearin decreeade.

G

Yeat wifelye (at laſt) calling to remembraunce
That Goddys fo workeinge ſhe ought not to refiſte,
Shee tooke it as thinge of Goddys ordynaunce,
And made as hee weare of her nowhit myſte ;
Ferdre confyderinge in Hym to confiſte,
As Hee her fent that fweeatiſte creature,
To fende an other at His owne pleafure.

[*f.* 19ᵇ.] Togeather they lyued certayne yeares after,
The numbre howe manye I cannot well geſſe,
Wheare God remembred his fervaunte *Walter*,
Sendynge by *Grifilde* a fayre newe encreafe,
A goodlye younge thinge, a Prynceſſe pearleſſe,
Whome, to bee Chriſtianed as folke did carye,
Her parentis wolde her to bee called *Marye*.

Of whiche noble Babe the Mother was fayne,
Father alfo, as right goode caufe had hee,
Withe all the Cowrte, bothe gentylman and fwayne,
And thorowe the Royalme was highe felycitee,
Withe prayfingis to Gód the moſte that myght bee,
Whiche well appeared, thoughe longe afterwarde,
They weare (in effeéte) of Hym that tyme herde.

For, longe tyme after, this noble Virgyn
Of all this whoale worlde proved the cheif flowre ;
The glorye of God ſhee did agayne begyn
That was as layde downe by dyuyllifche erroure,
And it eſtablifched, by Goddys helpinge powre,
In fuche fodayne and wondrefull faſhyon,
To all this worldys greate admyration.

Yeat, undreſtande yee, ere this pryncelye mayde
Was brought (as is ſaide) to her highe eſtate,
Neauer was Prynceſſe more ſoarer affayde
In taiſtinge ſorowes of wondrefull rate,
Ynowghe to haue geauen an vttre checke mate
Eauyn to the bardieſt that eauer was ſeene ;
God was her ayde, it cowlde not els haue beene.

But for on *Griſilde* oure mateir dothe depende,   [ſ. 20.]
And not on *Marye* pryncipallye tentreat,
Leſte I myght happen be thought to offende
Throughe Adulation, a meddeler muche great,
I will thearfore nowe (chalengeinge no cheate
In ſorte ſuche wiſe of commendation)
Ferdre of *Griſilde* heere make relation.

¶ *Of* Griſildis *vpp tradinge her goodlye younge Prynceſſe ;
Of her ſyngular towardnes to all vertue howe this
Royalme (that ſeaſon) floriſched in moſte highe honour
and felicite ; and of this* Griſildis *godly perfeɛtion, to
thexample of all noble women euyn to the worldys ende.*

¶ *Caput* 4.

*RISILDE* enioyinge this virginal floure,
And ſhee receauynge Puryfication,
She had it nuriſched in her owne bowre
Till tyme was come of ablaɛtation ;
Then tooke ſhe on her muche theducation
To have her traded in honorable ſorte,
Of whiche I am not heere hable to reporte.

But thus muche we dare heere boldely to wright,
She brought her vpp withe all dylygencye
In all kynde of vertue ſomuche as ſhee myght,
To Goddys dwe honour moſte ſpeciallye ;
As ſhe encreaſed to knowledge more hye,
So dyd goode *Griſilde* for her ſtill prouyde
To haue her foſtred as chicke by her ſyde.

[ſ. 20ᵇ.] Shee had to her ſorted men well expert
In Latyne, Frenche, and Spaynyſche alſo,
Of whome, before they from her did reuert,
She gathered knowledge, with graces other mo ;
The thynge atchieued departed her not fro,
For, as ſhee had promptnes the thynge to contryue,
So had ſhee memory paſſinge retentyue.

Emonges her inſtruᶜtours, before other ferre,
Highely floriſcheinge in the Latyne tonge,
She had the famous *Thomas Lynaker*,
Whois rules for her remaynethe vs emonge,
Throughe whome in Latyne ſhe ornatlye ſpronge,
Whiche afterwardys, bearing domynation,
Was vnto her moſte highe conſolation.

For none theare was that had withe her to dooe,
Straunger or other, what ſoeauer he was,
But his demaundys ſhe cowlde anſweare vntoo,
And geue graue ſentence in moſte profounde caſe ;
So wiſelye for her good *Griſilde* dyd purchace
That no kynde of vertue ſhe dyd wante,
But weare withe her lynkte as in couenaunte.

This *Walter* and *Gryfilde* fuche wife indude
Withe this mofte godly and towardys iffue,
Betweene whome afterwardys, heere to conclude,
Was neauer moe, their ftyrpe to contynue ;
But as to rype age this more and more grue,
So trulye fhee, withe beawtye decorat,
Dyd paffingelye floryfche in her eftate.

By longe tyme after *Walter* and *Gryfilde*   [*f.* 21.]
Their lyues they ledde in highe felicitee ;
His will (mofte gladly) fhe alwayes fulfilde,
By all that laye in her poffybylytee.
In Brytayne that tyme was muche tranquyllytee,
Plentye of althyngis in computation
That ferued (of neade) to mannys fuftentation.

The honour of God duelye florifchinge,
His feruyce mayntayned eauerye wheare,
The riche the pooare right gladlye nurifchinge,
The greateft (at ftreffe) biggeft burdayne to beare,
To that was godlye each leanynge his eare ;
So decent ordre was not then ouer all,
But after it had a muche fodayne fall.

Of which I will not (at this tyme) heere faye,
But tawke of *Gryfilde*, that foueraigne wight,
Whoe ordred her life fo godlye alwaye
That none cowld euyl her, fayinge but the right ;
The loue of God was alwayes in her fight,
Before thyngis worldelye ynwardlye caftynge
To pleafe the Lorde that was eauerlaftynge.

Her almes to the pooare was ample and large,
None came to her gatys withe oute refreſcheinge ;
To her Almoſyner ſhee gaue in charge
To bee dylygent in dyſtrybutinge,
Moſte ſpecially to haue á reſpeçtinge
To the ympotent, aged, and ſuche,
They (before other) moued her harte muche.

[*f*. 21ᵇ.] This godlye pytee ferdre had ſhee
In townys and villagies, neare wheare ſhe laye,
She wolde (ſecreatlye) ſende to goe ſee
To knowe wheare neaded her almes to conuaye ;
Some ſhurtys, ſome ſmockes, ſome certaigne monaye,
Or what thynge els was thought they dyd neede,
As ſhe perceaued ſo ſholde they ſure ſpeede.

Sometyme wolde ſhe ſende ſecreatlye alſo
To weeite wheare the pooare weare layde in childe bed ;
Knowinge thearof, ſhe wolde herſelf ofte goe,
And cauſe to bee brought bothe ale, beeare, and brede,
Candyll, and ſuche thynges that myght doo them ſtede,
Bothe ſheeates and lynen leauynge theare behynde,
Withe alſo monaye other neeadys to ſynde.

She was not quoyſche, diſdaynefull or prowde,
But cowlde be pleaſed to vyſite the pooare ;
Withe God thearfore ſhe was highely alowde
And after (withe fauour) let yn at His doore ;
Thoughe heere agaynſte her Hee let the wynde ſtoore,
It was the more to her ſowlys ſalvation,
For heauyn is woonne by muche trybulation.

This godlye maner ofte wolde fhee frequent
At *Greenewiche*, fhe lyinge alone from the Kynge;
The Fryers at matyns withe hartye entent
She wolde bee theare, in devotyon kneelinge,
A mantyll aboute her whiche was no riche thynge,
Theare in prayer and contemplation
Renderinge to God fweete commendation.

All was her harte in holyneffe pight,   [*J.* 22.]
Thoughe in this worlde yeat not of the fame,
In worldely.thynges fhee had no delyte,
For whiche in heauyn is regeftred her name;
To that onlye ende fhe fullye dyd frame,
As all that eauer her fafchyons knwe
Can yeat recorde my fayinge to bee true.

And for the deuotion fhe fpecially had
In the remembraunce of Chriftes Paffion deere
(Her fpyrite, ynwardely, to comforte and glad)
An ymage, that reprefentation beere,
She dyd let make, in wondreful manere,
Vpon á mownte á lyttle from *London*,
Befydys the waye goynge to *Iflyngeton*;

Not to any ydolatryall entent
(As myferable men manye dothe holde)
But to the beholders to reprefent
Of Chrifte towardys man the mercyes manyfolde.
Her feruencye in vertue cannot bee tolde,
For ftudiouflye fhee neauer dyd ceafe
But day by daye in vertue to encreafe.

Ferdre, yeat more of her goodnes texpreſſe,
Thoughe ſhe from *Brytayne* weare an alyan,
This was moſte true, witheoute all doubtefulnes,
Aboue all nations ſhe loued an Engliſcheman,
And dyd for manye as well proued than ;
And I for them thus muche agayne will ſaye,
They loued her withe all that in them laye.

[ſ. 22ᵇ] When ſhee on Progreſſe in the ſomers tyde
Roade with her *Walter* themſelfes to ſolace,
Wheare they did come the Countrey farre and wyde
· Wolde thycke aſſemble to beholde her face,
Cryinge á mayne " Chriſte ſaue her noble grace,"
Withe ſecreat tawlke her highelye commendynge
Aſmuche as they wolde dooe *Walter* their Kynge.

Beſydis all this, this moſte excellent Queene
A ſyngular zeale had vnto learnynge,
As bothe in *Oxforde* and *Cambrydge* was ſeene,
In mayntaynynge lectures, and Scholars helpeinge,
With manye a gyſte to the Churcheſſe aydinge ;
What thynge was neadful to vertues pleaſaunce
She was moſte readye to dooe her furtheraunce.

The gratious deadys of this worthye woman,
Whiche are well knowne to ſundry yeat lyuynge,
And ſhall neauer dye by all that I can,
If thearto maye helpe my ſymple wrytynge,
All to entytle paſſethe my cunnynge,
But for ſomuche as to my knowledge came
I haue, and ſhall, gladlye ſet furthe the ſame.

¶ *Howe* Walter *fought meanys to bee dyuorced from* Gryfilde *his wife ; howe his Counfelours (for feare) then
fhranke from the truthe ; of the great Cardynall* Thomas
Wulfaye; *alfo of* Anne Bullayne, *on whome* Walter *fet
fpecially his harte, her as to marrye in goode* Gryfildis *fteade.*

¶ Caput 5.

FTER with*Walter* her foueraigne lorde   [*f.* 23.]
She had beene matched nye twenty yeares fpace,
The curfed Enemye, fower of dyfcorde,
Began to fue his accuftomed trace,
Goode *Gryfildis* eftate for to difface,
Mofte wickedlye that anye can difcuffe ;
All, for fhe was to hym contraryous.

Some wycked theare weare, at his exitation,
(To picke a thanke of hym their foueraygne)
That prompted *Walter* after this fafhyon ;—
For that *Gryfilde* was fo longe tyme barayne,
Wantynge a Prynce his name heere to mayntayne,
That he thus fholde, as for that purpofe, make
Her to geue upp, and fome younger to take.

Or whither it came of his owne headye mynde,
(As certaigne it was he wolde bee fenfuall),
It fhall not (at this tyme) of mee bee dyffynde,
But furthe the mateir I profequute fhall.
This motion muche laye in his memoryall,
Sore occupied thearin bothe daye and nyght,
For muche it was pleafinge to his appetyte.

H

Ferdre, to mayntayne his fonde opynyon,
Falſe Flaterabundy to hym drewe neare,
Enſenſinge hym after this condytion,
That muche more kendeled hym in the matere,
For that ſhe was wife vnto hys brother,
Whearby he had moſte juſte occaſion
To make of her a ſeparation.

[ſ. 21ᵇ] Theis twoe pryncyples broached in ſuche wiſe
Walter his Counſell counſeled thear vpon,
Whoe, perceauynge his earneſt entrepriſe,
Condeſcended to his purpoſe anon :
They durſte not (contrary) ſpeake their reaſon,
He was ofte tymes ſo rageinge furyous,
Whiche, in a Prynce, was tomuche pyteous.

Halaſſe! that Counſelours in any caſe
Shoulde ſhrynke oughtis their headys to ſpeake in the right!
Halaſſe! that Prynces ſholde ſeeme to lacke grace
To ſuffre flaterers to byde in their ſight!
Whoe ſo that ſhrynkethe the truthe to recyte
When eauer hee bee demaunded his mynd
Is but a flaterer in vearye kynde.

If Pryncys wyllis maye haue no denyall,
But, as they wyll, their wyllys to take effecte,
What neade theare then bee Counſelinge tryall
Or anye Counſelours (at all) electe,
Sithe, at their wyllys, they will take or reiecte?
As goode no Counſell but they herde may bee,
And better none then hyde the verytee.

A Counſell (of olde), as hathe beene telled,
Is choaſen, and ſet, to ordre á kynge,
And ought not (throughe forſe) to bee compelled
But as true juſtice appoyntethe the thynge,
Takynge fundation on this olde ſayinge,
Twoe wytts (or moe) to bee better then one ;
So they to termyne, and not one alone.

Whye are they choaſe of the auncyent ſorte   [ſ. 24.]
But for their wiſedome and godly prudence ?
The younge ̨addyng wytts returned á torte
For that they lacke the like experyence.
If then in them bee wylfull neglygence,
In caſe of truth to woorke contraryous,
They ſhall ſure rue their deade vngratius.

So nowe the Kynge withe his Counſellis conſent
Hathe fullye determyned in this caſe ;
Gryſilde, whyther ſhe wyll or no bee content,
She muſte (no remedye) reſigne vpp her place,
Theare was for her no other maner grace ;
Of whiche manye light braynes weare ioyous and glad,
But oother godlye moſte ynwardelye ſad.

The younkers (lyke lackwyttes) hoapeth nowe faſte
To ſee this ſodayne alteration,
Fooliſchelye bleatynge owte many a blaſte,
Of vayne wytleſſe communycation,
Vndre this ſorte and braynſycke faſhyon,
" Nowe ſhall wee ſure haue ſome goodly younge ſeade,
When *Walter* is gone, to reigne in his ſteade ;

" Nowe ſhall this ſure feche bee feched aboute,
To haue ſome freſche Prynce ouer vs to reigne,
So ſhall all countreyes of vs ſtande in doubte,
And of oure fauours to bee glad and fayne,
Whiche neadys to this Royalme muſte purcheſſe great gayne;
So ſhall oure Kyngys mynde in quyet bee ſett,
When he to the ſame ſome younge peece ſhall gett."

[*f.* 24ᵇ.] Thoughe light kyttiſche wyttys lyſted to ſaye ſo,
Olde, prouydent, ſobre, wiſe and dyſcreete,
They wyſte it ſholde breede muche ymmynent woe
If ſo goode *Gryſilde* weare caſte vndre feete,
Depryued her Crowne, whiche was farre vnmeete ;
The caſe ſecreatly ſo conſyderynge,
Bycauſe they coulde not remeady the thynge.

*Thomas Wol-
ſey Cardynall* At that ſelfe ſeaſon in *Brytayne* theare was
A certayne great and myghtye *Cardynall,*
Whoe was of Counſell to brynge this paſſe,
A wycked man, a vearye Belyall,
Puffed withe pryde moſte paſſinge ſpeciall,
Whoe (certaynly) witheoute cauſe or ſkyll
Towardys goode *Gryſilde* beeare lytle goode wyll.

Hee counſeled (men ſaide) withe Aſtronomyers
(Or what other ſecte I cannot well ſaye,
Weare they Sotheſayers or weare they lyers),
Whyther he ſhoulde fall or floryſche alwaye ;
Whois anſweare was, he ſhoulde come to decaye
By meanys (they fownde) of á certayne woman,
But what ſhee ſholde bee they coulde not ſaye than.

Vpon whiche fonde enygmatization
Vnto goode *Gryfilde* ympute it dyd hee,
Whearefore in his imagynation
He wrought to haue her depofed to bee ;
But hee theare myftooke, it was not fure fhee
That fhoulde hym brynge to his fynall myfchaunce,
Goode *Gryfilde* neauer wrought anyes hynderaunce.

Yeat one theare was that brought hym to his bane,   [*f.* 25.]
And not goode *Gryfilde* as he dyd it take,
Whois pryncely honour nowe for to prophane
To *Fraunce* he can á coftelye journaye make,   1528
Wheare he for the Kyngis fyfter thear fpake,
Whiche mateir concluded to his entent,
Whome he repayred, as wife as he went.

Thoughe at his theare beeinge, as well it is knowne,
He fundrye other mateirs dyd entreate,
For greefys that towardys the Pope weare then growne
By themperour, for vrgeant caufes great,
At whiche this *Cardynall* tooke a great heat,
Yeat one fpeciall was to forefayde cafe,
In whiche hee wanted bothe wifedome and grace.

At tyme of canuafinge this mateir fo,
In the Cowrte (newe entred) theare dyd frequent
A frefche younge damoyfell, that cowlde trippe and go,
To fynge and to daunce paffinge excellent,
No tatches fhee lacked of loues allurement ;
She cowlde fpeake Frenche ornatly and playne,
Famed in the Cowrte, (by name) *Anne Bullayne*.   *Anne Bul-*
layne.

On her dyd *Walter* ofte caſte his frayle iye,
So ſtedfaſte and ſure, it myght not aſtarte;
To hym theare was no ſuche creature earthlye,
His loue was theare ſet neauer to departe,
Falſe Cupydo ſo ſtonge hym to the harte,
He thought vnto her theare weare no mo lyke,
Shee was to hym ſweete as balme aromatyke.

[ſ. 25ᵇ.] No lytle towardys her was hys longeinge luſte,
Oute of his preſence he cowlde ſuffre her ſcace,
At his commaundement ſhe daunce and ſinge muſte,
Only aboue all ſhee ſtoode yn hys grace,
Whiche ſundrye and many adnoted the caſe,
That well they wiſte they wolde togeathers knytt,
What ſoeauer lawe dyd oughtys prohybyt.

A Prynce his mynde onſe ſettynge on á thynge,
Beyinge as wronge as poſſyble to be true, -
Cauyllations ynoughe ſome wyll ſoone brynge
That to his purpoſe the thynge ſhall enſue;
So (at this ſeaſon) to frame for this Nwe
They laide to goode *Gryſilde* her ſterylenes,
Whiche ſhe cowlde not helpe; God ſendeth all increaſe.

And (peraduenture) to God maye bee knowne
Of His holye lawe ſome makynge but light,
For that in their owne lande their ſeade is not ſowne,
Theyr poſterytee He dothe it ofsmyte,
And heyres erectethe pleaſinge in His ſight;
Thoughe Kyngis to their myndys maketh muche thearfore,
Yeat God in their dooyngis wyll ſure haue an ore.

Ferdre they burdayned goode *Gryfilde* as thus,
For that to his brother fhe marryed was
Hee neeaded not to bee oughtys fcrupulus,
As nowe his enten (*fic*) to haue brought to paffe.
But of the mateir this was the uearye cafe,
Hee had in hym a lyttle fenfuall lufte
Whiche withe younge ware hee neadys accomplifche
       mufte.

His mynde fetteled on *Anne* in this wife,   [*f.* 26.]
She was aduaunced *Merquefe* of *Penbrooke* ;
As to their Queene, all dyd to her feruyce,
And like to Queene was her ftatelye looke ;
Howbeit, many myght her fcacelye brooke,
So lowe (as fhee) to clymbe fo fodaynlye
They feared to haue a fowle deftynye.

¶ *Of* Walters *ſendinge to* Rome *for a divorſment but none myghte bee obteyned, he takinge his Progreſſe (the mean while of his meſſengers returnynge) to* Grafton; *Of* Gryſildys *great patience in her aduerſytee; Of the Cardynal's fall, and the cauſes of the ſame, And of his penytent departure oute of this life at* Leyceſtre *Abbey.*

¶ *Caput* 6.

HIS peece pickte oute and choſen for the noanſe
Whearon *Walters* harte was earneſtly ſett,
Meſſengers to *Rome* weare ſent then attoanſe
A Diuorſment in all great haiſte to gett;
But this was thearof the veary whoale lett,
The *Churche* (throughe dwe proofe) to let them marrye,
The *Pope* (then beynge) wolde yt not contrarye,

In that muche grauelye hee thus conceaued,
The *Churche* to bee founde of ſuche duplycitee
Her credyte thearbye myght bee bereaued,
And ſchiſmys taryſe by muche enormytee;
Whearfore hee wolde not in anye degree
In this vrgent mateir graunte his conſent,
So myght bee obteyned no Dyuorſment.

[*ſ.* 26ᵇ.] *Walter,* ſuppoſinge his purpoſe to haue ſped,
The tyme of his meſſengers paſſage to Rome
To *Grafton* Maner his Progreſſe he dreſſed,
Till they (in this caſe) brought hym the Popys dome.
So into Northamptonſheere hee did come,
The nwe *Merqueſes* withe hym in like caſe
Withe huntynge paſtyme themſelfys to ſolace.

The goode fealy *Gryfilde* was thear alfo,
Withe muche heauye harte and pyteful cheare,
Not in eftate as fhe was wonte to go
But oute of fauour, fhe ftandynge á reare,
Ofte fecreatlye fheadynge manye á falte teare;
Withe ynwarde fighyngis fecht from the harte roote,
For that whiche (vtterlye) was then no boote.

At her wolde *Walter* cafte no chearful looke,
Nor fhe durfte approache near to his prefence;
Hee cowlde her not in anywife then brooke,
Nor fhe (as Queene) to woorke anye pretence,
But, as an abiecte, ftandinge in fcilence,
Geauynge attendaunce, withe harte fore pyned,
To what ordre fhe fhoulde be affigned.

Thoughe heauynes her harte did ouer loade
For tomuche vnkyndenes fhewde to the fame,
In perfecte charitee fhee alwayes aboade,
And thanked God howe eauer it dyd frame,
Withe wifedome frayltee thus ofte to blame,
Howe eache true Chriftyan it dothe behooue
To fuffre trobles for Chriftys deere looue.

Afmuche as fhe myght fhe kepte her felfe clofe   [f. 27.]
Within her chamber in oratyon,
In whiche her defyre and vtter purpofe
To God fhe had in commendation,
As to ordre to His contentation,
Confirmynge her felfe withe all obeyfaunce
To His pleafure and dyuyne ordynaunce.

I

At whiche ſelfe ſeaſon the *Cardynall* then
Attended on the Cowrte theare witheout fayle,
Not in pompe withe his numbre of men,
But as a dogge that had brent his tayle;
Illucke began hym then faſte to aſſayle,
Theare fewe or none had hym oughtys in reſpecte,
But was as one in maner cleane abiecte.

Noforſe whye wolde he goode *Gryſilde* deſpite,
He ſped the woorſe (I dare ſaye) for her ſake;
Whoe enuyethe the goode, God will hym requyte
Withe ſome mysfortune; example I take
[Pſ. vii. 15.] At theis *Dauythes* woordys, "Whoe diggethe a lake
Oother thearin (vngodlye) to entrappe,
Is take in the ſame by ſodayne myſhappe."

So this ſaide *Cardynall* lyttle before
Practiced goode *Gryſilde* for to depoſe,
And nowe of hym ſelfe hee can ſaye no more
But is as like his owne honoure to loſe,
Of whome ferdre I ſhall ſomewhat diſcloſe
(By honeſt credyble information)
Howe hee fell into trybulation.

[f. 27ᵇ.] Twoe cauſes theare weare as I haue herde tell
That greatly made to his confuſion:
A certayne younge lorde in his Cowrte dyd dwell
Whoe ſhewed pretence to this concluſion,
(Whyther of earneſt, other illuſion,
The veary certayntee ſcace ſaye I can)
For to haue macht withe the ladye *Anne*.

His lorde (the *Cardynall*) as hee thearof knwe
He raged withe hym outragyouflye,
Proteftinge he fhoulde his entreprife rwe
If eauer he herde hym vfe her companye ;
This was before fhe was ordayned ladye ;
Whiche from her knowledge was not kept fecret,
Whearfore longe tyme fhe muche ynwardlye fret.

Thother occafion was (as is faide) this :
When *Walter* on her dyd firfte cafte his mynde,
He afked the *Cardynall* what his aduyfe is,
Whoe anfwearde hym, as after [s]he dyd fynde,
She was not for hym in anye maner kynde,
Vnleffe for Concubyne he wolde her take,
But as his Queene her clearlye to forfake.

Of whiche twoe thynges as fhe had knowledginge,
Nowe that fhe is aduaunced vp fo hye,
She hathe them daylye in her remembringe,
And the *Cardynall* hated mofte fpitefullye ;
So dyd alfo *Walter*, ye well maye efpye,
At the *Merquefes* fecreat perfwafion,
For he was nowe cleane out of eftymation.

And ymmedyatlye after this Progreffe
He was called to a Computation,
Wheare, of his juellys, treafure and rycheffe,
Was to *Walter* made refignation ;
After whiche great extreme purgation
To *Yorke* (his See Churche) dymytted he was ;
His caryage was eafed, he myght lightlye paffe.

[*f.* 28.]

Yeat ere that he came to the ſayde cytee
(Throughe what occaſion I cannot well ſaye)
He was ſent after, withe great velocytee,
Towardys the Cowrte to haiſte hym furthe waye,
Whiche ſodayne nues put hym in mortall fraye ;
Notwitheſtandinge, withe muche trobeled harte,
Backwardys to *Leceſtre* he dyd reuert.

In whiche journeyinge by the wayes (doubtles)
Hee tooke certayne pyllys, his ſtomake to purge,
Replenyſched withe greuous heauynes
For this ſodayne tempeſtyous ſurge,
Ryſinge (as he thought) throughe the *Merqueſes* grudge ;
So that of neceſſytee by the waye
He tooke reſtynge at *Leceſtre* Abbaye ;

Wheare, thorowe woorkynge of the ſaid peelys,
(Whiche, as I herde tell, weare too too manye)
And thorowe ſorowe, hymſelfe he theare feealys
His life to forgoe witheoute all remeadye ;
No longe was the tyme while he dyd theare lye,
Not paſſinge eyght dayes at the veary moſte,
Tyll he was foarſed to yealde vpp the goſte.

[*f.* 21ᵇ.] Before he departed, right Chriſtyanlye
He ſent for the Pryor and was confeſt,
The Euchariſte moſte reuerentlye
Receauynge into his penytent breſt,
Aſkynge God mercye withe harte moſte earneſt
For that (in his tyme) by will, deade and thought,
Agaynſte His goodnes he had eauer myſwrought.

the Seconde.

And to fignyfie that hee was penytent,
Certaynlye, the Pryor I herde thus faye,
A fhurte of heare was his indument
Next to his bodye, when he thear deadde laye ;
For whome hartelye it behoaueth to praye,
Sithe hee heere ended fo penytentlye,
To whome (no doubte) God grauntethe His mercye.

What thoughe he lyued muche remyffyuelye,
Farre oute of the trade of his profeffion,
Yeat dyinge.(as hee dyd) penytentlye,
His fowle (no doubtys) hathe heauyns ingreffion
By hauynge in harte vycis fuppreffion ;
For, thoughe mannys life bee neauer fo infecte,
God (fpeciallye) his ende dothe refpecte.

Some he callethe in their enteringe eftate,
Some (certaynlye) in their adolefcence,
Some at the terme of their decrepyte date,
As this *Cardynall,* fo departed henfe :
Yeat, hoapynge of age, let none woorke offenfe,
Myndynge at that tyme his fynnes to forgoe,
Lefte deathe hym preuent ere hee can doo foe.

As happe hathe happened, pytee it was   [*f.* 29.]
That oute of fauour fodaynly he went
Before he (fynally) had brought vnto paffe
His entred purpofe, fo paffinge excellent,
His College in *Oxforde,* it may well bee ment,
Witheout (as it fhewthe) the full perfection,
Of whiche I fhall tell the caufe of erection.

¶ *The Occaſion of the Erection of* Chriſtys Churche *yn* Oxforde *by the Cardynall* Thomas Wolſaye, *the numbre of the woorke ffowlke, what he theare pretended; Of* Doctor Cockes (*Deane of the ſame*) *moſte dyuylliſche diſorderynge theare and of his alſo deſpoyſinge* [ſic] *the ſaide Churche and other in* Oxforde *to the mayntaynaunce of his fylthy and vyle carnalyte.*

¶ *Caput* 7.

T tyme when this man in highe fauour ſtoode,
Walter withe hym tawlkynge famylyarly,
A certayne gentleman withe muche ſobre
    moode
(As then a ſuetor) ſtoode theare á looif by,
On whome as *Walter* that tyme caſte hys iye,
He aſked hym, withe countynaunce benynge,
If that withe hym then hee wolde any thynge;

To whome the partye thus entred his ſute,
Beſeachinge his grace to graunte his lycence
A ſcholar of his, his ſchoole heere to permute
Beyonde the ſeayes, to dooe his dyligence,
For more acquyringe, by ſtudyes pretence,
Of lyterat knowledge for yeares twoe or thre,
The habler after to ſerue his Maiſtee.

At whois contemplation *Walter* furthewaye   [*f.* 29ᵇ.]
Condefcended to his humble requeft,
And to the *Cardynall* hee theare did faye,
" I merueyle whye oure folke are fo earneft
Their youthe beyonde feaye to haue entereft,
To the confumynge of oure Royalmes treafure ;
Haue wee not Scloolys [*fic*] them at whome to recure ? "

" Syr," (quoth the *Cardynall*) " pleafethe it your grace
Me to affifte in that I dooe pretende,
I fhall fo wɒorke in conuenyent fpace
As fafte hitherwardys to caufe them defcende
As eauer thitherwardys they did themfelfes bende,
And oother alfo of eache Chriftian porte
For the like purpofe hyther to reforte."

" My Lorde," (quoth *Walter*) " furdre your pretence,
Whiche is (I perceaue) fome ftudye to begyn,
And yee fhalbee fure of oure affiftence,
What waies fo eauer yee thynke befte thearyn."
Vpon whiche occafion hee dyd not lyn
(The plot deuyfed and curyouflye cafte)
To fet thearwithe in hande wondreflye fafte.

Mofte cunnynge woorkemen theare weare prepared,
Withe fpedieft ordynaunce for eauery thynge,
Nothynge expedyent was theare oughtis fpared
That to the purpofe myght bee affiftynge ;
One thynge (chieflye) this was the hynderynge,
The woorkefolke for lacke of goode ouerfeers
Loytered the tyme, like falfe tryfelers.

[*f.* 30.] They weare thus manye, á thoufande (at the leafte),
That thearon weare woorkeynge ftill daye by daye,
Their paymentes contynued, their labours decreafte,
For welneare one haulfe did noughtis els but playe.
If they had trulye done that in them laye
By fo longe fpace as they weare tryfelynge,
At his fall had beene lyttle to dooynge.

The warke was wondreful paffinge curyous,
And tomuche fet furthe to his vayne glorye ;
Tomuche it cannot bee to gloryous
To His honour that reignethe eternallye ;
Thother preferred, that beeynge layde by,
The warke cannot take profperous fucceffe ;
Of the godlye I take thearyn wytnes.

Theare fhoulde haue beene reade within that precynéte,
(To thinftruétion of all that thither came),
The feauyn Scyencies feryoufly lynkte,
As in their ordres the Schoolemen can name ;
The Readers to haue beene men of great fame,
The picked pureft throughe all Chriftiandome,
If meede or monaye myght caufe them to come.

But, howe eauer it was, Goddys ayde theare did lacke,
It had not els quayled, as yt fhewethe yeete ;
That Pryde thearyn hathe oughtys hyndered backe
I trufte Humylytee fhall perfeétlye compleete,
To fet vpp Goddys howfe, as mee feemethe meete,
For His ineftymable beneuolence
Shewde (of His grace) to her magnyficence ;

Oure noble *Queene Marye* it is that I meane,   [*f.* 30ᵇ.]
Whoe, as fhee is mofte noblefte nowe of all,
That noble warke not yeat fynyfched cleane,
Noblelye God graunte her to make yt formall,
To His honour and glorye fpeciall :
Her other affayres firfte brought to goode fyne,
God (throughe His grace) her harte thearto inclyne.

Pytie it weare but it fhould goe forwarde :
To furdre learnynge is merytoryous ;
By learnynge, to all that lifte not bee frowarde,
Is knowne to pleafe the Lorde mofte gratyous,
And to all fortys what duetyes becumethe vs ;
So that to thearof the true mayntaynaunce
All (to their powres) ought to dooe furtheraunce.

So haue wee heere faide the caufe orygynall
Howe *Frydifwide* howfe a Studye became,
By the great traueyle of the *Cardynall*,
Whois fowle God fheelde from the infernall flame,
And profpere in vertue the Studentes of the fame ;
They indeauorynge fo, vertuouflye,
No doubte to Goddys pleafure fhall muche edyfie.

Well I confydre (fymple thoughe I bee)
What worthie graces dothe learnynge enfue ;
Withoute learnynge and dwe cyuylytee
Man is not hable hymfelfe to refcue ;
Learnynge, whoe dothe yt perfeɛlye indue,
To eache degre, of all maner a fute,
Their pertyculars can well diftrybute.

K

[*ſ.* 31.]   Learnynge in cauſes to God appertaynynge
             (Whiche Reaſon tranſcendethe) can ſaye and perſwade,
             Howe by true Faithe Man haue muſte his aydinge,
             And not by Reaſon in althyngys to wade ;
             Learnynge inducethe the vearye true trade,
             To diſtrybution, as I note can,
             Of all that is due bothe to God and man.

             Then, worthye is learnynge of preferment
             And of all degreeis to bee magnyfied,
             For learnynge rendrethe the lowe excellent,
             And the excellent wyttye to bee tryed ;
             Learnynge and wiſedome togeathers allyed,
             As freendys and kynne of conſanguynytee,
             They neadys ſhall woorke to muche vtylitee,

             Admyxted withe grace, I meane, as noleſſe,
[1. *Cor.* viii, 1.]   For Scyence, Sainĉte *Paule* ſaithe, the mynde doth inflate ;
             Of Scyence hathe manye had plentyouſnes
             And voyde of Grace hathe proued farre ingrate,
             Vſynge their learnynge after dyuyliſche rate,
Of Doĉtor Cox.   As *Doĉtor Cockes*, withe á *Combe* thearto ſett,
             Throughe fleſchelye folye cawght in the Dyuyllis nett.

             Whois noyſome, curſed, and dyuylliſche ſubuertinge,
             By hym, as in his vttermuſte powre laye,
             Of godlye ordre, althyngis conſyderynge,
             From that was goode to the contrarye waye,
             I can none other wiſe of conſcience ſaye,
             To Vertue hee was an vtter enemye,
             As (to his ſhame) his faĉtes dothe teſtifye.

Abhorrynge his ordre of facrede Preeiftehod,   [*f.* 31ᵇ.]
A whoare hee tooke hym, wife cowlde he take none,
For contrarye vowe hee made vnto God
When of His Mynyfters hee tooke to bee one;
But for hee wolde not to the Dyuyl alone,
Hee wrought (by all meanys) other to entrappe,
Withe hym (for eauer) to curffe their myfhappe.

Hee wrought by his holye ftynkeinge *Martyr*   *Peter, the*
                                                                                              ftynking Mar-
Peter, that *Paule* his breathe cowlde not abyde,   *tyr.*
(For that, like Sathans true knyght of the Gartyr,
His holye doctryne hee heere falcyfide)
That whoe (of Preeiftes) in maryage was not tyde
Hee was afflicted, tormoyled and tofte,
To loffe of lyuynge or fome other cofte.

Somuche abhorred this vagynge verlet
All fignes of godlye conuerfation,
That whearefo a preeifte withe fhauen crowne he met
Hee fhooke hym vppe withe deteftation,
And in Oxforde his ordynation
Was, whoefo theare a crowne on hym dyd fytt,
His College he fhoulde for his crownys fake amytt.

This was á worthie famous Doctor,
This was á man worthie of preamynence,
This was á Chriftian true Profeffor,
This was á man of right intelligence;
The Dyuyl hee was! I faye my confcience,
He was (I faye) an erraunt curfed Theeif;
His actys declare, yee neade no ferdre preeif.

[*f.* 32.] Hee robbed the Churche of *Frydyſwis* (I ſaye)
Of Chalyces, Croſſes, Candylſtickes withe all,
Of ſyluer and gylte, bothe preacious and gaye,
Withe Coapis of tyſſue and many a riche Pall,
Dedycat to God aboue æternall ;
And other Collegis maye hym well curſſe,
For thorowe hym they are farre yeat the wurſſe.

Hee was choaſe *Chauncellor* for fawtes amendinge ;
Hee mended (indeade) from goode to the badde !
Hee was a *Chauncellor* of the Dyuyls ſendinge,
Neauer was Towne that ſuche an other hadde ;
So made hee ordynaunce, that á prowde ladde
Withe men right reuerende myght ſhewe hym checkmate,
And went dyſguyſed yn ruffyan rate.

Hee ſet them all cleane oute of diſcyplyne,
And ſawe them ſetteled in heynous hereſye ;
Hee let them (at will) wickedlye inclyne,
He nothynge to vertue dyd edyfie,
But what to goode ordre was contrarye ;
So wrought hee, that (trulye), to make reporte,
As the *Deane* was, ſo weare the more ſorte.

So I wiſche not *Frydiſwiſe* to floriſche
In ſorte as that *Cox* example theare lefte,
But true ordre of Scholars taccompliſche,
Of whiche (wyckedlye) he ſawe them berefte,
Suchewiſe indued and withe grace fullye feſte
As, nowe I theare noate, by ſignes I doo ſee ;
I wiſche their furtheraunce the moſte that maye bee.

¶ Walter *fynyfchynge his* Progreffe, *paffinge thorowe* [f. 32ᵇ.]
Thame, *and other Townys, the newe* Merquefes *fafte
by his fyde, what mutteringe the* people *had on* Grifildis
partye and for her doughter Mary. *The Meffengers
reuerte from* Rome *without Dyuorfement ;* Walter (*by
a wycked man*) *was moued to take vpon hym the Supreamacye ouer the churche of* Englande.

Cap. 8.

OR all our tedious and longe dygreffion,
We haye not forgote oure former pretence ;
Walters pleafure fulfilled at *Grafton*
To *Buckingehamfheere* he drefte hym from
thenfe,
At *Ixill,* before the deeare fell to offenfe,
To fynyfche that tyme his huntynge feafon,
For Holye Roode Daye was then pafte and gone.

From thenfe wheare hee came, fafte iumpe by his fyde,
Accompayned hym the ladye *Anne Bullayne,*
All pleafaunte, frefche and gallaunt that tyde,
Goode *Gryfilde* followinge, as one of her trayne,
At whiche manye (that wife weare) did difdayne
So noble á woman to bee forfake,
And in her fteade fo meane á thinge to take.

For thorowe *Thame*, that gentle Merket Towne,
The Kynge then iſſued vpp to *London*warde,
Wheare dyuerſe and manye their headys henge downe ;
To ſee the caſe, withe *Gryſilde* howe it farde,
Vnto their hartys, God wote, it went full harde,
And thus did ſaye, mutteringe as they ſtoode ſtill,
" Chriſte ſaue goode *Gryſilde* to His bleſſed will."

[ʃ. 33.] " O Lorde !" (they ſaide, togeathers as they ſtoode),
" What meauethe our Kynge goode *Gryſilde* to forgoe,
Whiche hym heere followethe withe trobled moode,
That better for her weare ſhe weare ferdre froe ?
In his ſolacinge ſhee feelethe but woe ;
Whoe can her chalenge or blame in the caſe,
Shee to followe an other in her place ?

" Shee (bleſſed womon, God comforte her harte !)
Hathe beene full godlye and louynge withe all,
And her behaued in eauerye parte
Moſte honorablye, bothe to great and ſmall,
And nowe her honour thus wiſe to appall !
To ſpeake in the caſe wee maye nother dare,
Yeat pytee it weare ſhee ſhoulde oughtes mysfare.

" What hathe ſhe tranſgreſte to bee thus caſte owte,
A Queene (of bloode) ſo excellent as ſhee ?
Of her behauyour none neadethe to dowbte ;
Some bale is bruynge, what eauer it bee ;
Straunge is this ſight whiche wee heere nowe ſee,
A Queene moſte royall to come all behynde,
And ſo meane before ; this gothe oute of kynde.

"Well, well," (they faide) " God graunte all proue well !
Wee feare fome ftraunge nues fhall after enfue :
If fo á kynge maye his wife thus repell,
(So goode á woman and full of vertue),
Of weddelocke joynynge farewell then, adue !
This example, if it thorowly frame,
Shall other enfence to practice the fame.

" If their unytinge had beene thought wrongefull,   [f. 33ᵇ.]
Whie fo longe tyme contynued haue they ?
His Father (of witt and wifedome not dull)
What myght, and myght not, before did purveye.
Profpered togeathers they hathe many á daye,
And wee in wealthe and muche tranquyllytee ;
This is noughtys els but Mannys fragylytee.

" This is noughtis els but Mannys fenfuall mynde ;
God graunte wee all haue not caufe to repent !
Let hym not looke á newe better to fynde,
Reafon withe reafonable ought bee content.
Fye ! that at that age Man fhoulde bee infolent !
For, without all maner of fufpection,
This is begone of carnall affection.

" Wheare is become fage Difcretion as nowe,
In fuche noble Peearys that ought to frequent ?
Wheare is vnto God his duetye, as howe
To haue in awe His holy commaundement ?
Thoughe hee it let flippe in his inwarde entent,
Hee mufte and fhall make anfweare in the cafe
When powre, nor felfe wyll, fhall rowte in the place.

" God graunte hee (cheeiflye) repent not this geare,
For neadys it muſte breede great inconuenyence,
Thoughe whiche wayes wee knowe not, howe, when,
    or wheare ;
The ſoare of this paſſethe oure intellygence.
For *Dauyths* treſpace, oppreſt withe peſtylence,
Thouſandys of his abode the afflicſtion :
Synne, ſore of Kyngis, ſtoorthe Goddys maledicſtion.

[*ſ.* 14.] " But ſithe his affecſtion is nowe ſo ſett,
And the mateir ſo earneſtlye begoone,
Wee (poore Subjecſtes) maye it in nowiſe let,
But feele it wee ſhall, by althynges bee doone ;
Raſche recheles luſt his race will neadys roone,
Like cowlte vnbrydeled, reaſon depryued,
Throughe ſhame (in fyne) moſte ſtraungely diſguyſed."

Suche, of the rude and pooare Comynaltee,
Was (ſecreatlye) their tawlke and whiſperinge,
Whoe vnto *Gryſilde* beeare loue and feualtie
Withe all that in their pooare hartys was lyinge ;
And ferdre, they had this careful ſayinge,
" Halas I if *Walter* goode *Gryſilde* denye,
What ſhall become of her doughter *Marye ?*

" What ſhall become of that pryncely Flowre
That all this Royalme hathe joyed ſo longe yn ?
Shee ſhall forgoe then her Pryncely honoure ;
The weyes thearvnto wee ſee dothe begyn.
None only but God maye oother grace wynne ;
For Mother and Doughter what ſhall beetyde ?
Wee can but praye Chriſte for them to prouyde."

This of one Towne was not only the tawlke,
Or of one Countie, Cytee, or Burrowe,
But comonlye, wheare eauer men did waulke,
This noble Royalme (in maner) cleane thorowe,
So deepe in their hartys it graued furrowe ;
For they of wyttie confyderation
Feared tenfue great dyffipation.

But what aduayled their tawlke in this cafe ?   [*f.* 34ᵇ.]
It dyd their goode wyllis but as fignyfie ;
The mateir dyd then but paufe for a fpace,
Tyll from *Rome* the Meffengers myght them hye ;
Walter, nowe fetteled wheare he wolde lye,
His expectation (daylye) then was
To heeare nues, howe his purpofe came to paffe.

By this the Meffengers to the Cowrte came,
Voyde of the purpofe for whiche they weare fent :
So foone as *Walter* vndreftoode the fame,
For malencolye hee ynwardelye brent,
And was (throughe malice) mofte earneftlye bent
Agaynfte the Bufshope for fayinge hym naye,
Ragynge as lyon depryued his praye.

At whiche felfe feafon one certayne ftoode by,
Whois name (thoughe I herde) I will not expreffe,
Whoe faide to *Walter*, muche coragyouflye,
" What fhoulde this mateir oughtes vex your highnes ?
Ye maye (witheoute doubtinge) it clearlye redreffe ;
Sithe yee are heere Kynge and lorde of this lande,
Yee dooynge youre lyfte, whoe dare youe witheftande ?

L

"Yee, takynge on youe the Supreamacye
As headde of the Churche ouer all Brytayne
And other youre Domynyons ſpecyallye,
Yee maye (at pleaſure) then althinges ordayne,
So foreauermore *Rome Cowrte* to refrayne ;
If yee not ſticke to put this in practice,
Whoe is that dare denye youre entrepriſe ? "

[ſ. 35.]   *Walter* this heearynge his harte can reuyue,
Callynge to hym of his Counſell the cheeif,
For the ſaide mateir withe ſpeede to contryue
That hee weare quyeted oute of his greeif ;
The thynge by Perlyament putten in preeif,
It was condeſcended after his mynde,
None durſte ſay naye but Deathe hee liſte to fynde.

¶ Walter *fendethe to* Oxforde *to haue his cafe difcuffed,*
John Longelande (*Bufshoppe of Lincolne*) *his cheif Commyffioner, Fryer* Nicholas *Defendaunte in the fame, Fyue
Inceptours,* Doctors, (*withe fundry other*) *fpecially witheftandinge thearin, wheare* Women *fhewed them felfes on*
Gryfildys *Partye; Thunyuerfiteis* Seale (*by ftealthe*)
goaten; And what myferyes enfued.

Cap. 9.

EAT, for that *Walter* wolde not be thought
   (Of headye poure) to woorke contrariouflye,
   Hee fent to *Oxforde,* as playnnes he fought,
   To haue his cafe theare tryed by the
      Clergie,
At whiche trauelynge certaynlye was I,
Attendynge vpon a certayne goode man,
Whearfore in the fame I fomewhat faye can.

Thither was fent as cheeif Commyffioner
The *Bufshoppe* of *Lincolne,* one *John Langelande,*
Withe certayne other that well cowlde flatter,
The learned judgment theare to vndreftande,
Wheare one *Fryer Nycholas* took muche in hande,
As cheeif Defendaunte in the forefaide cafe,
Whoe fownde hym felfe macht euyn to the harde face.

[f. 35ᵇ.] But theare was vſed no indifferencye;
Suche as by learnynge made againſt the Kynge
They weare redargued moſte cryellye,
Threatened alſoe to forgoe their lyuynge;
On thother ſyde, all thearto inclynynge
They had highe chearinge withe meede otherwaye;
Falſehod tryumphinge, Truthe quakynge for fraye.

That tyme an Acte theare ſhoulde haue gone forwarde,*
Wheare Seauyn famous Clarkes that Inceptors weare
Bycauſe (in this caſe) Fyue wolde not drawe towarde,
It was dyfferred, to their heauye cheare,
For that their cheeif freendys weare preſentlye theare,
Mawdelaye, Mooreman, Holyman alſo,
Mortimer, Cooke, withe other Twoe moe.†

Theis Fyue in nowiſe wolde graunte their conſentes,
The Regent Maiſters weare of the ſame mynde;
Rather, they graunted to forgoe howſe and rentes
Then weetinglye ſo to ſhowe them ſelfes blynde;
The Proctors, for gaynes they hoaped to fynde,
(Throughe frendeſhippe they made) obteyned the grace
Of *Buſhoppe Langlande* the Acte to take place.

---

* "Note that an Act was ſolemnized 8 Apr. 1530, being the ſame day that the Univerſity inſtrument for the divorce was dated. The Doctors that then ſtood in the Act were Richard Mawdlin, archd. of Leyceſter, John Moreman, William Mortimer, John Holyman, Robert Cooke, Robert Aldridge, and Thomas Charnock, a Dominican."—*Note by Ant. à Wood to his extract of this paſſage:* Wood *MS.* (*Bodl. Libr.*) D. 18, part ii. fol. 72.

† "Aldridge and Charnock, that did readily conſent."—*Ibid.*

The mateir longe tyme theare hangynge in fufpenfe,
Witheoute hauynge Thunyuerfiteis feale
As to confyrme *Walters* forefaide pretence,
For whiche the Bufshoppe harde threatnynges did deale,
To his reproache, and hynderaunce of goode heale ;
If fo that fome theare had had hym at large,
I wolde of his life haue taken no charge.

For on the outegatys* wheare hee by nyghtes laye   [*f.* 36.]
Wear Roapes fafte nayled, withe Gallowes drawne by,
To this entent, as a man myght well faye
" If wee fo myght, fuche weare thye Deftynye."
His feruauntes ofte handeled accordynglye,
As, one (indeade) makynge water at a wall
A ftone (right heauye) on hym one let fall.

Women (that feafon) in *Oxforde* weare bufye,
Their hartes weare goode, it appeeared noleffe ;
As *Fryer Nicholas* chaunced to come by,
" Halas !"(faide fome) " that we myght this knaue dreffe,
For his vnthankefull daylye bufynes
Againfte oure deeare Queene, good *Gryfilidis* ;
Hee fhoulde euyl to cheeaue, he fholde not fure myffe."

Withe that, a woman, (I fawe it trulye,)
A lumpe of ofmundys let harde at hym flynge :
Whiche myfte of his noddle, the more pytie,
And on his Fryers heelys it came trytelynge,
Whoe (fodaynly), as hee it perceauynge,
Made his complaynte vpon the women fo,
That thirtye the morowe weare in *Buckerdo.*

* " Of Lincoln Coll."—*Ant. à Wood, ut fupra.*

Theare they contynued three dayes and three nyghtes,
Till woorde was ſent downe from *Walter* the Kynge,
Whoe fret at the harte, as vexed withe ſprytes,
That *Griſildys* parte they weare ſo tenderynge,
To all that ſo dyd, this woorde downe ſendynge,
That, magre their teeathes, hee wolde haue his furthe,
And ere longe tyme make ſome of them ſmall wurthe.

[*ſ.* 36ᵇ.]   But yeat for all that the Fyue foreſaide Clarkes,
Withe moſte of the Regent Maiſters, that tyde,
For all the threatnynges that flaterers barkes
From that was the right they wolde nowhit ſlyde.
The *Buſſhoppe Langelande* dyd thus then prouyde,
A Conuocation of certayne to call,
And gote the Seale as conſented of all.

For whiche was weepinge and lamentation,
I was then preſente and herde their complaynte :
" Halas ! " (they ſaide), " in pyteful faſhyon
Nowe is goode *Oxforde* for eauer attaynte !
Thowe that haſte floriſched art become faynte !
Thowe weare vnſpotted till this preſent daye,
Withe truthe euermore to holde and to ſaye.

" But notwitheſtandinge, conſyderinge as thus,
Thoue weare withe powre and myght ouerlayde,
Thoue thearfore remaynyſte innoxius,
As dothe (by vyolence) the rauyſched mayde.
Eaueriche his duetye on eache pate bee payde,
That is, whoe of vs hathe wronged the right,
God to their deſertes their dooynges requyte.

" This to this ende wee put in remembraunce,
To the knowledge of oure pofterytee,
That all, that feafon, made not dyffemblaunce,
But tenne to one ftucke to the verytee,
But cheife that ought had no fyncerytee ;
Falfe Ambition and Keepynge yn fauour
Declared in this muche lewde behauour."

In this mateir is to bee adnoted   [f. 27.]
What euyl counfell withe Pryncys maye induce,
For, confequentlye, this Royalme was forted,
As water breakynge ouer hedde or fluce :
All goode ordres weare cleane fet oute of vfe,
Suche calamyteis enfuynge theare vpon,
To this Royalmys neare fubuerfion.

Then florifched Flatery tryumphantlye,
Then Falfehod beeare rule, and Truthe fet á fyde,
Then weare the goode maligned throughe enuye,
Then was true Meekenes ouercome withe Pryde,
Then to perdition all Goodenes fafte hyde,
Then was Selfe wyll cheif Ruler ouer all,
Then myght, in right, none for Aduocat call.

Then of the Churche began thaffliction,
Then entred Herefies curfed and nought,
Then encreafed Goddys malediction,
Then His due honour in great decaye brought,
Then the goode not regarded as they ought,
But euery Ribaulde myght them checke and chace ;
The Goode depryued, the Badde in their place.

In earthe they cowlde not their malice extende,
But vnto heuen ſhewed indignation ;
The holye Saynctys theare they dyd diſcommende
By too too muche abomynation,
Sclaunderinge certayne vndre this faſchion,
Howe holye Virgyns, of no lyttle ſome,
Weare Concubynes to the Buſshoppe of Rome.

[ƒ. 37ᵇ.] The gloryous perpetuall Virgyn *Marye*
No better eſteamed then an other woman ;
Eache doungegell as goode as the Sanctuarye ;
Theis myſcheifes, withe hundredefolde moe, began
At the incummynge of this nwe Queene *Anne*,
Whoe, as ſhe was, declared at the laſte,
Whome God vanyſched withe muche ſodayne blaſte.

As good and bleſſed inducethe Vertue,
And woorkethe all meanys to mayntayne the ſame,
So the malignaunte dothe Vertue ſubdue,
Bycauſe their doyngis ſhee dothe fierſlye blame ;
Prooif whoe ſo notethe, Vice endethe withe ſhame.
Then was no wondre this alteration
To breede great meanys of deſolation.

For, certaynlye, vpon this induction
Entred in this Royalme ſuche innouation
(To the pooare mannys vttre deſtruction),
Rayſinge of Rentes in wondreful faſhion,
From one to fyue in ful numeration,
To cawſynge of dearthe in vytayl and warys,
Withe other ſundrye ineuytable carys,

Somuche the bodye not heere moleftynge,
But hundredfolde more endaungeringe the fowle ;
At Faftynge and Prayinge was made but ieftinge,
The vile Ignoraunte the Clarke to controwle,
All holye cerymonyes coniuringe the Mowle,
Eache cockynge Cobler and fpittyllhowfe Proctor
In learnynge taken fo goode as the Doctor.

In tokne yeat more of Infidelytee,   [*f.* 38.]
Downe went the Croffes in eauerye countraye,
Goddys fervauntes vfed withe muche crudelytee,
Dyfmembred (like beaftes) in thopen highe waye,
Their inwardys pluckte oute and hartis wheare they laye,
In fuche (mofte greuous) tyrannycall forte
That to to fhamefull weare heere to reporte.

Shortelye after, to mende the mateir more,
Churches and Monafteries downe they went,
To haue the treafure fpeciallye thearfore,
Althoughe they fayned for other entent,
After this Prouerbe, to like confequent,
The Glouer (craftelye) brought this reafon yn,
The Dogge to bee madde, all to haue his fkynne.

Yeat this was not the vttremufte euyl ;
Theye nybbed Chriftes faithe after their pleafure,
So weare they ledde by their Maifter the Deuyl,
For, on the truthe, they lyed oute of meafure :
The whoale heere to wright I haue no leafure,
But to this ende I haue reherfed this,
What came by exchaunge of good *Grifilidis.*

M

¶ *Walter ſendethe to* Gryſilde *to reſigne vp her Crowne, whiche ſhe neauer wolde graunte ; Of her wondrefull and wyttye anſweare ; She is ſecluded the Cowrte ; What complaynte ſhe made for her Doughter* Mary, *and of her greeif for her* Mother *agayne ; Howe* Walter *wolde bee ſeene to dooe vpryghtly, and all vnrightlye (in this caſe) hee wrought.*

¶ *Caput* 10.

[*f.* 38ᵇ.]

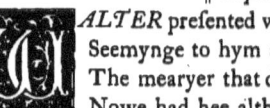ALTER preſented withe Thunyuerſiteis Seale,
Seemynge to hym all had condeſcended,
The mearyer that daye he made his ful meale,
Nowe had hee althynges as hee pretented.
Forwardys hee went, hee was not defended,
The goode ſealye *Gryſilde* for to put downe,
And in her ſteade his nwe mynyon to crowne.

At *Brydewell* (his place) that ſeaſon hee laye,
And theare was alſo goode *Gryſilidis ;*
Thoughe in his preſence ſhee came nyght nor daye,
Shee muſte theare attende, his pleaſure ſo is ;
To whome hee ſent then, by certayne of his,
Her Crowne to reſigne, of foarſe ſhee els ſholde,
Whiche playne ſhee denyed, vſe her as hee wolde.

Shee ſaide, to hym ſhe was true wedded Wife,
All Chriſtendome ouer can wytnes the ſame,
So wolde ſhee acknowledge duryinge her life,
Howe eauer otherwiſe hee pleaſed her to name ;
As for his owne Royalme, for feare they did frame
To the fulfillinge of his fixed mynde,
Witheout reſpe&inge what Conſcience dothe bynde.

Shee added, his Father was thought man of wytt
And wyttelye he wrought ; whoe lifte, his actys vue ;
All Chriftian Clergye alowed them to knytt ;
If they vnknytt them, fhe wolde yt not rue ;
But vntill fuche tyme fhe wolde contynue,
Witheoute confentynge to refignation,
Howeeauer hee beeare her his indignation.

Ferder then fo, fhe merueyled greatlye   [*f.* 39.]
They lyuynge fo longe in looue and vnytee,
And was withe her pleafed, as dyd fignyfie,
Till latelye, what eauer the caufe fhoulde bee,
She hym obeyinge withe all humylytee,
Alfo neauer dyd, other pretended,
Whearwithe his courage myght bee offended.

Or if fhe had beene an Adultereffe,—
Of whiche all the worlde cowlde her not accufe ;
She was towardys hym knytt withe all ftedfaftnes,
Withowte (in that kynde) anye maner brufe,
Whearfore the more it made her to mufe
So noble a man, fo wyttie withe all,
Into fuche an opynyon to fall ;—

Or if hee cowlde faye, or anyman els,
That owghtys for her fake hee had mysfared,
In his propre Royalme or owtewarde trauels ;—
But God for hym had freendelye prepared
As in his affayres neauer oughtys fquared,
By myfaduenture, to greeif of his Eftate ;—
Then caufe myght feeme her to bee repudiat.

For in Adultery whoe ſo ioynethe,
Hee maye bee ſure to bee infortunat;
No luckye ſucceſſe God hym aſſignethe,
But is withe myſcheeiſes manye intricat;
So hathe not (throughe her) happened hym euyl fate,
But tryumphauntly, in pryncelye degree,
Floriſchinge in wealthe and felycitee.

[*ſ.* 19ᵇ]   Concernynge the ſterylnes layde vnto her,
It was witheout reaſon, diſcretion or ſkyll;
She had, and moe myght, thorowe due order,
Haue borne and brought furthe, to anſweare theartyll;
But luſte at lykynge his luſte dyd fulfyll:
(Meanynge, hee elſwheare diſperſed his ſeede,
Whearfore God wolde not more ſeade to proceede.)

So made ſhe anſweare, this noble woman,
At ſendynge to her her Crowne to reſigne,
Withe muche moe reaſons then I rehearſe can,
For ſhe was lyghtened withe grace dyuyne;
But by no maner meanys ſhe wolde inclyne
Her Crowne to ſurrendre for weale or woe,
Thoughe *Walter* neauer maligned her ſo.

Whiche anſweare, as *Walter* dyd vndreſtande,
Hee tooke the mateir muche furyouſlye;
As one that had all the lawe in his hande,
Hee wolde her ordre as cauſe hee ſawe whye;
Commaunde then did hee, in his fell furye,
Oute of his Cowrte theare ſhe ſholde be conueyde
To wheare he aſſigned, theare to bee ſteyde.

So was goode *Gryſilde* ſecluded the Courte,
Aſſigned (as Warde) whyther to reſorte ;
Yeat worſte thynge of all, whiche did her moſte hurte,
Her deareſte Doughter from her was holden ſhorte ;
One myght not an other (in care) comforte ;
The *Mothers* harte ſomuche it dyd not byte,
But (trulye) the *Doughters* it did as deadly ſmyte.

" O Lorde," ofte ſayde this godlye *Gryſilde*,   [ƒ. 40.]
Withe tearys (nodoubtys) of ynwarde penſyuenes,
" Wolde to God my *Walter* weare thus well wylde
My *Doughter* and his, that is as Prynceſſe,
That I myght ſee her, to eaſe my dyſtreſſe ;
Thoughe he ſo farre liſte to bee ouerthwarte,
She weare ynoughe to recomforte my harte.

" She weare ynoughe to my contentation,
That I myght ſee in ſtate howe ſhe dothe ſtand,
Whyther ſhee bee in like trybulation,
Caſte oute of fauour, from ſtate, goodys, and lande,
As certaynly my mynde bearethe mee ſo in hande ;
Thoughe (peraduenture) not yeat as am I,
I feare (ere longe henſe) the Feendys fallacye.

" I feare, and myſtruſte, for mee (her Mother)
She ſhall (at all) fare nowhit the better ;
Thoughe God wolde none bee wronged for other,
Muche ſundrye wayes Sathan the goode can fetter ;
Whoe dare from eyther conueye oother letter,
Though Reaſon and Nature wolde graunte theare till,
Yeat falſe malignours wolde rayſe thearof yll.

" I am no Traytores, I let all men weeite,
No more is my *Marye*, I dare proteſt ;
Wee are moſte readye to all that is meeite ;
Whye then ſhoulde anye vs wrongefully moleſte ?
Whye may not bee had this rightfull requeſte,
The *Mother* and *Dowghter* togeathers bothe twayne,
Agreeued á like, theyr greefis to complayne ?

[*f.* 40ᵇ.]　" I cowlde bee content, and ſhee (I dare ſaye),
(If *Walters* goode will wolde graunte to the ſame)
To lyue togeathers yn ſome pooare Nunraye,
Prayſinges to rendre to Goddys holye name,
The quyeter to lyue, oute of this worldys blame ;
For, fye on this worldys highe Domynation
Commyxte (in this ſorte) withe trybulation !

" Whye was I joyned to ſuche highe Eſtate,
And thus repelled withe hate and diſdayne ?
Whye not rather to ſome of meaner rate,
That myght of mee (as I of hym) beene fayne ?
Whye thus it prouethe, what ſhoulde I complayne ?
Geeue mee my Doughter, I holde mee content ;
Wheare reſtethe the fawte God graunte amendement."

Suche complaynte (ſyttinge all ſolytarye)
Goode *Gryſilde* wolde ofte vnto herſelfe make,
Prayinge to God for her Doughter *Marye*,
That Hee of her the gouernement wolde take ;
Muche was ſhee careful (in harte) for her ſake,
No Mother eauer was heere, oather yendre,
That, more then ſhe dyd, myght her childe tendre ;

Whoe at that feafon, as Pryncefſe foueraigne,
At *Ludlowe* kepte howſeholde muche honorablye ;
Hearinge her Mothers vexation and payne,
Vnto her harte it went moſte paſſinge nye ;
Thoughe ſhee (deeare mayde) cowlde it not remeadye,
She prayed nyght and daye, withe many a teare,
The heauynlye Father to helpe in this geare.

Shee faide, (as ſhe ſpeciall occaſion had),   [*f.* 41.]
"O myghtye *Jeſu*, maker of althinge,
My Mother, dolorous, penſife and fad,
Thowe (in her forowes) bee ay comfortinge,
Turnynge the harte of my Father the Kinge
Her otherwiſe (of gentlenes) tentreat,
And not taſffliɛte her withe forowes fo great.

"If (as dothe feeme) his purpoſe take effeɛte,
To geeue her vpp, aſſumynge the other,
Mee alſo withe her hee fure will reieɛte,
Aswell the Doughter as fo the Mother.
O God ! fende helpe, the better the foner !
Or, in Thye fight if it bee fo decreed,
Welcome thye will ! I am right well agreed.

" Welcome what wayes foeauer Thowe liſte aſſigne !
Befeachinge Thy magnyficent goodnes
In nowiſe wee bothe oughtys to maligne
(Throughe frayletye of mynde) for worldely diſtreſſe,
But, to receaue it, all due meekenes,
As fent by Thy dyuyne operation,
For (as Thou knowiſte) fome confyderation."

Suche was this princelye maydyns prayer daylye ;
Somuche the Mother had her not in mynde
But the Doughter aſmuche her ſemblablye,
So mutuallye wrought Nature of kynde ;
But *Griſilde* at *Walter* no fauour myght fynde,
Reproched ſhe was by vtter contempte,
As from his fauour and companye exempte.

[ſ. 41ᵇ.] Muche was in this caſe Walters ſolycitude
He wolde bee ſeene all to frame vprightlye,
And all vnrightlye he wrought to conclude ;
So was hee blynded in his fantazye,
Hee was ſelfe mynded muche meruelouſlye,
So that on what thinge his mynde was onſe ſett,
He wolde haue his furthe, he wolde haue no lett.

¶ *Walter commaundethe a Cowrte at* Dunſtaple *wheare*
Gryſilde *was depoſed from her eſtate* ; *Of this worlde and
ſignyfication of the ſame* ; *Why* Gryſilde *withſtoode her
Reſignation, whoe was geauen to name* Lady Douager ;
*howe Pryncys, faylinge their Faithe, geauethe occaſyon
to other to dooe the like, for whiche this Royalme hathe
beene* (*and is*) *moſte greuouſly afflicted.*

Caput. 11.

ERCEAUYNGE as *Walter* did perfectly well
Thanſweare of *Griſilde* concernynge her
Crowne,
No worthynes had beene her to compell,
Whiche, weyinge and ponderinge, made hym to frowne,
Yeat neadys (withe ſpeede) he wolde haue her put downe,
Althoughe witheoute reaſon, ſkyll or offenſe ;
Shee was not hable to make reſiſtence.

Immedyatlye then enſuynge all this
A Cowrte he aſſigned at *Dunſtaple,*
To whiche was ſummoned goode *Gryſilidis*
To make ſuche anſweare as ſhee was hable ;
But what thearyn was oughtes profitable ?
Howe muche goode right ſhe eauer did diſcloſe,
Hee was at á poyncte to haue his purpoſe.

[*ſ.* 42.] Theare at that Cowrte was toſſinge and turnynge,
To ſmall goode effecte wheare right ys compelled,
For durynge the tyme of the Judgis ſoiurnynge
At goode *Gryſilde* they greuouſlye ſwelled ;
What ſo herſelfe or her Proctours telled,
It was witheoute all eſtymation,
The mateir had earſte determynation.

The mateir was earſte deciſed as thus,
Anne Bullayne Gryſildys place to ſupplye,
And *Gryſilde* to *Walter* repudius
Bycauſe ſhe was not pleaſinge to his iye ;
What ſhoulde they then lenger tyme occupye ?
Judgement followed, before contryued,
So was goode *Gryſilde* her place depryued.

So was the goode and godlye reiected,
For that to this worlde ſhe was not pleaſinge ;
So was the other in place elected,
Bycauſe to this worlde ſhe was contentinge :
[St. John, The worlde louethe his, by Chriſtys owne tellinge,
xv. 19.] And his enemyes hathe in illuſion,
As heere nowe prouethe the concluſion.

This worlde is bothe blynde and phantaſticall,
Fycle and falſe in all his practycinges,
Inconſtante, muche praue, and perylous withe all,
Of whiche to bee ware wee haue great warenynges,
Hee ſo deceauethe by ſundrye compaſinges ;
Whois notoryous reprehenſible ſtate
To certayne entent wee ſhall dyuulgat.

The Worlde is the People, it is no leaſinge,   [ƒ. 42ᵇ.]
The greater parte, by innumerable ſorte,
Geauen to peruerſe and wrongeful dealinge,
Farre oute of trade whiche Goddys truthe dothe exhorte,
To lye, to ſclaunder, to gawde, and to ſporte,
To fleſchlye alſo abomynation,
Withe other meanys of muche deception.

Takinge to name *Worlde* of the People ſo,
Bycauſe all worldelye their faſhions dothe frame,
Of whiche ſaid Worlde the Dyuyl (our mortall foe)
Is cheif Capytayne, Chriſte grauntinge the ſame,
" The Prynce of this Worlde, in his furyous flame,   [St. John,
Commethe to ſeeke lucre, in Mee hathe hee none ; "   xiv. 30.]
For Hee was not of this Worldys condytion.

Nomore was this godly *Gryſilde* trulye,
In worldelye pleaſures ſhee had no delyte,
Aboue, the heauynlye Manſion on hye,
Was firmelye fixed her whoale appetyte ;
Thearfore this Worldys Prynce had her in deſpyte,
And, at his curſed exitation,
The Worlde did her all this vexation.

What more vexation myght vex her harte
Then wrongefullye ſo entreated to bee,
Depoſed (as to ſaye) from her dwe parte ?
Not ſeene the like, in ſuche nobilitee,
So highe, to deſcende to lower degree,
Onlye by ſurmyſed inuaſion ;
No ſmall thearfore her greeſes occaſion.

[ƒ. 43.] Whye fhee witheftoode or made refiftence,
And was not willinge her ftate to forgoe,
Confyderinge farre higher preamynence ·
For wronges fufteynynge belonge fuche vnto,
She for this caufe did fpecyallye fo,
In right to ftande behouethe all and fome,
Euyn vntill Deathe the life dothe ouercome.

Another as this vndreftande wee maye ;
Shee (beeinge á woman of great prudencye)
Confydered, in her Depofition laye
Daungers occulted, open to her iye,
Deftruction of Chriftys Sanctuarye
Withe hundred other calamyteis mo,
If fhee her Eftate reiected weare fro.

Shee fawe Newfanglenes entred her foote
And was withe *Walter* famyliar to muche,
Alfo Herefye, of myfcheif the roote,
Newes to induce that dyd the quycke tuche,
In forte (as to faye) mofte horryble, fuche
That, if they weare not (in tyme) refifted,
To late fhoulde bee to haue them defifted.

For that, (like woman of godlye meanynge),
Shee was mofte lothe her Eftate to auoyde,
Confyderinge as howe parties weare leanynge
This Royalme thearbye to bee forelye anoyde,
Grace and Vertue, as creatures accloyde,
Weare heauye and fadde, as laboringe withe greeif,
For they themfelfes fawe geauen ouer of the Cheif.

In this to helpᵉ and fynde fome maner ftaye
This mercyfull Matrone manfullye ftoode,
Rather then womanlye to fhrynke for fraye,
Onlye of entent to dooe this Royalme goode,
That from her olde dwe began to chaunge moode,
As to chaunge honour, renowne and goode fame,
For difhonour, folye and flefchelye fhame.

Suche was the meane of this godly woman,
But God permytted the Dyuyl to take place
As ofte Hee fo dothe, probation prooue can,
When wronge is fuffred the right to oute chace ;
So oure defertes deferued in the cafe,
That of this woman vnwoorthye wee weare,
Whiche nowe at *Dunftaple* depofed was theare.

Depofed fhee was as feemed to the worlde,
But fhee exalted in fauour of the Higheft ;
Of longe the wicked mofte weywardely jorlde
Tyll whome they mynded to *Walter* was nygheft ;
O wicked worlde ! thoue wrongefullye wryeft,
So contrariouflye to affix thy looue !
Note well heereafter what thearebye fhall prooue.

When fo they had doone the thynge they came for,
They gaue her to name *Ladye Douager*,
A name leffenynge muche deale the honor
That of forne promyffe was due vnto her :
From Faithe when Pryncys begynnethe to erre,
Whiche other (their Subjeſtis) tobferue fhoulde fee,
What, in that cafe, of right then judge maye wee ?

[_ſ. 44._]　What is it but they the like will enſue?
And ſo dyd ſundrye, I feare not to tell,•
Gaue vpp their olde wyues and tooke them to nwe,
Makynge as nothynge of Chriſtys Goſpell;
A meanys that muche conduced vnto hell,
Whiche, at the headys, example ſo takynge,
Scace yeat at this daye hathe clearly ſlakynge.

So weddelocke not ſhynethe as I wolde wiſche;
God graunte ſome meanys of reformation!
To muche Adultery dothe ſtill floriſche,
As thearin cheeif their deleƈtation,
Witheoute feare of Goddys indignation;
I meane no ſmall Byrdys of the ſymple ſorte,
As preſidentes ſhewthe, dothe Rumor reporte.

For whiche, and other abomynations,
This noble *Brytayne* hathe beene plaged ſore
Withe ſundrye and manye trybulations,
I thynke no Royalme in Chriſtendome more.
Oure purpoſe otherwiſe tendinge, thearfore,
Thearto accordinge, proſequute we ſhall,
Till iuſte occaſion maye thearto befall.

¶ Gryſilde *depryued her honour was aſſigned too* Bugden, *the Buſshoppe of* Lincolns *maneir, whoe was cheif mynyſter of all her ſorowes, whear ſundrye her olde cheif officers and ſeruauntes weare commaunded from her ; Of her lamentable taking her leaue at them, and of her greuous complaynynge for* Walters *vnkyndenes towardys her.*

Caput 12.

THIS godly *Gryſilde* depryued her place,   [*f.* 44ᵇ.]
· To chaunge of cheeare not ſole of her alone,
(Whoe had cheif cauſe, conſyderinge the caſe),
But to the greeif alſo of manye á one,
After her wrongefull Depoſition
She was (as warde) from place to place conueyde ;
Leaſte to her comforte, theare was ſhee lengeſt ſteyde.

Place had ſhee none of her owne to reſorte,
Rentes or Reuenues digne to her eſtate,
Or oughtes that ſerued her ſpeciall comforte,
But beinge blanked as one all amate
(As was no merueyle, ſerued in ſuche rate)
Was commaunded to á place called *Bugdayne.*
In Huntingedone ſheeare to reſte and remayne ;

Whiche to the Buſshoppe of Lyncolne dyd belonge,
Whoe firſte began her heauynes to broache,
In á Sermon whearin hee waded wronge
And ſtoored, whearbye the breache did approache ;
At hym takynge light manye dyd encroache,
(For meede and promotion) that *Walter* myght
Exchaunge good *Gryſilde* and dooe but the right.

Vndre his handys her greeifes they grewe muche,
Whiche all to expreſſe ſhoulde ſeeme tedyous ;
Partely at *Oxforde* it was her chaunce ſuche,
Partely at *Dunſtaple*, as this dothe diſcuſſe,
And nowe was ſent to ſoiourne in his howſe ;
Alſo he was, emonges other thynges all,
The Executor of her Funerall.

[ƒ. 45.] That, of all noatys that I dooe adnote
Whiche hee (of his partye) to her did extende,
Was cheiflye the beſt, I all men behote,
For then weare her trobles brought to an ende :
I will not ſaye they dyd her thither ſende
For any coarſey vnto her ſtomake,
As ſome (peraduenture) wolde it ſo take,

But theare ſhe was for á certayne ſeaſon,
Wheare this other affliction her befell,
Which ſoundethe (me thynkethe) farre oute of reaſon,
As one of her Seruauntes to mee did tell ;
Her Offycers, that longe withe her did dwell,
Weare her auoyded for certayne entent,
And newe aſſigned at *Walters* comaundement :

At whois departure, when they tooke their leaue,
At her (their olde and reuerende Miſtreſſe)
Tendrenes of harte her powres did bereaue,
As tearys from the ſame did playnlye expreſſe,
Sayinge vnto them in her great heauynes,
" Halas ! youre ſeruyce to mee of longe date,
That I (no waies) can oughtes remunerat !

" Halas ! that (of forſe) I neadys muſte youe forgoe,
And yowe alſo mee ; no reamedye theare is ;
No lyttle thearfore is my inwarde woe !
What ſhall me nowe betyde I wote not I wiſſe !
Newe muſte I neadys take ; what meanethe by this
But of my tyme heere the ſhorte abrydgement ?
Whoe cannot reſiſte muſte holde her content.

" What is it for mee, or other the like,   [*f.* 45*ᵇ*]
Thoſe to forgoe (my Seruauntes moſte truſtie)
That in my cheeif neadys weare my whoale phyſike,
By fyrme affyaunce that in them had I,
All ſtraunge and vnknowne their romethes to ſupplye ?
It mouethe mee my life haulfe to fuſpecte,
Whither they are ſent the ſame to infecte ?

" For well I perceaue and vndreſtande maye,
Some are that ſmall paſſethe of my welfare ;
Weare I henſe rapte to morowe or to daye,
The ſhorter my tyme the leſſe wolde they care.
As abjecte, or thrall, they keepethe mee bare ;
And nowe of my Truſtie depryuynge mee,
What can they ſhewe of more extremytee ?

" But, for I muſte neadys obedyent bee,
I will in goode parte take as God ſhall ſende,
Prayinge youe hartelye to praye for mee,
As I ſhall for youe vnto my lyues ende ;
And ſo to God I humblye youe commende."
Whearewithe, to certayne (withe many a ſalte teare)
She gaue in rewarde of her wearynge geare.

o

So departed they eyther from other,
Withe muche heauye hartes as cheare dyd declare,
Throughe whiche her ende approached the ſoner,
As is a preparatyue Sorowe and Care;
What thearto myght make, ſome liſte not to ſpare;
Ynowhe was her trybulation in vre,
More then ſome euyn of the meanyſte myght endure.

[ƒ. 46.]   Her ſourgynge ſorowes (certaynlye), I ſaye,
So daylye encreaſte by muche abundaunce,
That thre yeares ſpace, witheout any delaye,
It had withe her á ſtill contynuaunce;
So was ſhe plunged in peruerſe peanaunce,
As, in degre, eſtate withe payne to cownte,
All greeis (of her gree) herſe farre did ſurmounte.

Emonges whiche all, this one did her ſore payne,
The Pooare to her repayringe for releeif,
And them (as ſhee wolde) not hable to ſuſtayne;
It was to her an inwarde deadlye greeif,
And to her enemyes á ſhameful repreeif
So goode á woman, and noble withe all,
To bee ſo vſed and holden in thrall.

"Halas!" ſhe wolde thus often tymes complayne
Vnto her ſelfe muche lamentablelye,
"Why dothe my *Walter* at mee thus diſdayne,
And I hym tenderinge, withe all feruencye,
For hym my life to put in ieoberdye?
No woman can wiſche her huſbonde more well,
Thoughe hee of mee can ſcante byde to heeare tell.

" Hee cannot fuffre mee neare his prefence,
Hee lifte not to fende to weeite howe I doo fare,
Hee fequeſtrethe mee from all preamynence,
Hee nowhit for mee dothe oughtes cure or care ;
Hee dothe to mee that hathe beene feene' but rare,
To caſte mee off, his true defpoufed wife,
And feemeth as foarye to heeare of my life.

" I deeme euyl counfell dothe leade hym in this ;   *[ſ. 46ʰ.]*
God fende hym better ! I can nomore faye ;
So noble á·man great pytee it is
That fo feduced fhoulde wandre á ſtraye ;
His deade to forthinke onfe come fhall the daye,
When nother I oughtes maye eafe his entent,
Nor hee to haue tyme to woorke amendement.

" What fhoulde I oughtes grudge or troble my mynde
For that whiche I fee theare is no remeadye?
To fhue to the worlde it weare but waiſte wynde ;
To God I appeale, That fittethe moſte hye ;
Hee is the Judge that judgethe rightuouſlye,
The wronged to meede of mercye tafcende,
And the offendre throughe grace to amende.

" Hee is Hee onlye in Whome I full truſte,
This worlde I defye withe his fautours all,
Not for that (of forfe) I neadys nowe fo muſte,
Bycaufe I am as thruſten to the wall
And bootethe not for remeadye to call,
But am beſte pleafed, fithe God will the fame,
To bee thus forted in forte as I am.

" Small deale mee mouethe my Depofitiop,
Whiche nothynge hyndrethe to my faluation ;
But wheare the fawte is I wifche contrition,
For ferdre fallynge in flagellation
Engendred by Goddys great indignation,
Thorowe makynge light of His holye lawes,
Setteled in fynne, defendinge theyr cawes ;

[f. 47.] " In whiche I wifche amendement right gladlye,
And not reuengeaunce that God fhoulde oughtes take,
But, thorowe His grace, demurely and fadlye
For flefchelye folye his confcyence to quake,
Throughe mouinge thearof his fynne to forfake ;
This is of all my cheeif petytion,
To voyde the wayes to fowle perdition.

" For thoughe falfe Frayletee foolifchelye voltethe
Into the feate of vyle Carnalytee,
And fo agaynfte mee the dooare hee boltethe
Witheoute all right and dwe vrbanytee,
I, not fetteled in fuche kynde of prauytee,
Befeache to all my malefaƈtours
In heauyn withe mee to bee contraƈtours,

" Theare in vnytee, withe one harte and mynde,
Æternally to geeue laudation
To the Redeamer of all mankynde
For oure heauynlye coadunation,
Notwitheftandinge this worldys variation,
Oure reconcylement wrought by dyuyne grace,
That wee maye (by Chrifte) inhabyte that place."

Suche of this godlye and bleſſed woman
Was vſuallye the meditation ;
She dreſte not her ſelfe to curſſe, other banne,
But tooke in goode worthe her conſtellation,
Lamentynge (rather) the diſſipation
Of thynges inſurginge to Englandys vndoinge,
Then in her cauſe the wrongefull myſuſinge.

¶ Gryſilde *remoued from* Bugden *to* Cowemolton, *wheare,*   [*f.* 47ᵇ.]
viſited wjthe ſicknes, ſhe felte her tyme come to departe
this life ; Of her moſte Chriſtian preparinge for the ſame ;
Of her moſte charytable takynge her leaue at Walter *and*
all other Nobles, Knyghtes, Gentlemen and Commoners,
deſyrynge them all to praye for her.   .

Caput 13.

FTER a ſeaſon, to *Walter* pleaſinge,
She had ſoiourned at *Bugden* foreſaide,
She was remoued, to more diſeaſinge,
To á towne *Cowemoulton,* theare to be ſtaide ;
As Walter wolde, ſhe helde her well ápayde,
Remembringe howe by murmuration
Was greatlye ſtoored Goddys indignation.

Awhile as ſhe had contynued theare,
God viſited her withe certaigne ſicknes,
Wheare thorowe greatly abated her cheare,
And more and more genderinge in proceſſe
That tyme was come to fyne heere her progreſſe,
Whiche, well vndreſtandinge her mortall ſore,
Moſte Chriſtianly ſhe preparde thearfore.

For bodelye Phyfike fhe nowhit cured,
But rather wifched to bee diffolued,
Of heauynlye ioyes to bee affured,
Whiche, after this forte, fhe ofte reuolued,
That, thoughe in the earthe her corps weare dolued,
Her fpyrite myght to the heauyns attayne,
As in her creation God dyd ordayne.

[*f.* 48.] To walke that waye as true Chriftyan ought,
Sauflye and furelye witheoute impedyment,
(Thorowe hoape in Hym that dearlye her bought,)
Shee firfte became á perfecte penytent,
Callinge to mynde her life muche negligent,
In whatfoeauer her confcyence cowlde mooue
Tochynge offenfe ágaynfte God abooue.

Then to the worlde fhe dyd her conuerte,
Her practycinges heere callynge vnto mynde,
Forthinkinge muche, withe á forowful harte,
That more then fhe ought fhe thearto inclynde,
Accufinge her felfe for creature vnkynde
Vnto her Lorde, that no darkenes may dymme,
That eauer this worlde fhe preferde before Hym.

Of Hym (mofte meekelye) fhe mercy befought,
Withe tearys oute tryllynge of pure contrition,
Grauynge His Paffion deepe in her thought
For her cheif garde againfte perdition,
Befeachinge thearby to haue remiffion
Of her offenfes venyall and deadlye,
Onlye and cheiflye for His great mercye ;

Remembringe this Texte, in her aduifement,
Howe, crauynge of God remyffion of fynne,
Behoauethe all men, withe conftant confent,
Vnto their neighbours the like to begyn,
Thearby the rather Goddys mercye to wynne,
Whiche nowe fhe hathe in confyderation
The more to make, for her fowlys faluation.

Thearfore fhe made this proteftation,   [f. 48ᵇ.]
" O *Jefu*, my Lorde and foueraigne Kynge,
Forgeue Thoue my fynnes abomynation,
As I forgeue all men me oughtes tranfgreffinge
By woorde, woorkynge, or wrongefull fuppreffinge,
And, as I wolde Thy heauynly affuraunce,
So graunte it them (Lorde) in contynuaunce."

Then this goode *Gryfilde* to make althinges fure
Her Gohoftely Father to her dyd let call,
To whome her whoale life fhee playne did difcure ;
To walke the waye that was vnyuerfall,
The gatis heere of Deathe that all men paffe fhall,
Depured alfo withe the Bodye of Chrifte,
Mofte commonly called the Eucharifte ;

Withe fuche deuotion receauynge the fame
As neauer myght woman poffyble more :
No figne of vertue myght any one name
But in her was feene, withe other great ftore ;
Life in her yeat reftinge, tell I fhall thearfore,
Howe of this worlde fhe tooke nowe her farewell,
As Chriftian affection did her compell.

At *Walter* (her lorde) ſhe thus wiſe began,
" Farewell, deere Huſbonde, to whome I was heere knytt
In lawefull ſpouſayle, as God ordayne can,
By His holye Churche, I playne confeſſe itt,
' And ſo I take thee tyll Deathe prohybit ; '
Farewell, withe full affectyon of harte,
For tyme is nowe come I neadys muſte departe.

[ƒ. 49.]   " Nowe muſte I walke the waye that thow muſte go,
Nowe maiſte thow marrye, impedyment is none ;
Nowe, that thy true wife is parted thee fro,
Thow mayſte bee free from fornycation ;
God wyll of thy ſynne the mytigation,
God wyll that I nowe, to ceaſſe thy treſpace,
Shall vnto thy choyce reſigne vpp my place.

" God ſende the mercye and goode ſucceſſion,
Withe proſperous reigne and peace contynuall ;
God in thy doynges bee thy direction,
As to thy ſowle healthe moſte cheifly make ſhall ;
This is my wiſche before my funerall,
Lynkte vnto thee by true Chriſtian looue
Whiche neauer (but Deathe) ſhall any remooue.

" My ſowle vnto God I only bequeaue,
My bodye wheare thowe ſhalte pleaſe to aſſigne ;
Aboue grownde I truſte thowe wilte it not leaue,
To be deuowred withe vermyne or ſwyne,
For that it was onſe vnyte vnto thyne,
Somuche the rather in Earthe it tengraue,
Thoughe other fauour I boote not to craue.

" But that I maye haue (as Reafon fo wolde,
For that I am of Chriftian beleeue)
Honeft intierment as Chriftian fholde,
Withe charytie delte, the pooare to releeue,
To praye for my fowle that may them fo meeue,
This I befeache thee, as pooare woman maye,
Voyde of all frendefhippe (faue.God) at this daye.

" Befeachinge thee ferdre, of nature and kynde,   [f. 49ᵇ.]
Thy Doughter *Mary* to cafte not awaye,
But that in thy fight fhe may fuche grace fynde
To be as thy Doughter knowne an other daye,
Sithe of thy bloode fhe is cummen nonaye ;
Not for my fake I moue to thee heere yn,
But for fhee is mofte neareft of thy kyn.

" Sithe God hath fent her to lyue in this life   [fic.]
And is of towardyfnes not to bee abhorde,
Thoughe mee thoue lifte not to take as thy wife,
Yeat bee thoue to her thus fpeciall goode lorde,
To fome ftaye of lyuyng to-fee her reftorde,
For that (as I faide) fhe is of thee fpronge,
And not for my fake to take the more wronge.

" Sore I myfdoubte her entretaynynge ;
If thoue renounce her for Doughter of thyne,
No fmall fhalbee her caufe of complaynynge ;
So teachethe the ftory of *Magubryne* ;
Let fomewhat thy harte towardys her inclyne,
For the deeare Bloode that from Chriftes fyde came owte,
For fhee is thy bloode, thoue neadift not to dowbte.

P

" And nowe to thee I haue nomore to ſaye,
But Jeſus take thee in His protection ;
To Deathes áreſt I neadys muſte obeye,
Whoe hathe in me powred his infection,
My ſowle to walke to Goddys election ;
Farewell thearfore for eauer and eauer,
For nowe is the tyme I muſte dyſſeauer."

[ſ. 50.]   Of whiche her ſaide mynde and fynall farewell
(As ſundry dothe ſaye) a Bill ſhe let make,
It ſendinge to *Walter*, that playnly dyd tell
The ſome thearof, howe eauer hee dyd it take,
Whoe ofte thearon thought, thoughe lyttle hee ſpake,
As afterwardys occaſion had hee,
By tryinge this worldys falſe duplycitee.

And, certaynly, for certayne tyme after
He was muche ſad, ouer he was wonte to bee ;
Some certayne remorſe moued in *Walter*,
By woordys in her Byll that wryten had ſhee,
So was it conſtrued of ſundry degree ;
Of whiche I wyll heere no lengre tale make,
But, takynge her leaue, howe ferdre ſhe ſpake :—

" Farewell, my Freendys, that wolde me oughtes well,
Jeſus rewarde youe wheare I am not hable !
Farewell, my Foes, wheare eauer yee doo dwell,
God vnto youe all bee mercyable !
Farewell, my Seruauntes, ſo ſeruyable,
That longe hathe ſerued vnrecompenſed,
God from all euyll ſee youe ſauſe defenſed !

" Farewell, bothe Lordys and Ladyes of eftate !
Farewell, yee Knyghtes and Gentlemen alfo !
Farewell, yee Commoners in hartyeft rate,
That hathe beene eauer me louynge vnto !
God I befeache Hym youe mercy to doe !
Farewell yee all ! my panges they are right fore,
Praye for my fowle nowe, I afke youe nomore."

Thus takynge her leaue mofte Chryftyanlye,   [*f.* 50ᵇ.]
In loue and charytee withe eauery man,
Yeat abydˆinge in perfeƈte memorye
An other Adieu fhee after began,
Afwell as her powre that feafon ferue can,
Vnto her deareft Doughter *Mary*;
So as I herde tell declare it fhall I.

¶ *Of* Gryfildys *mofte pytefull takynge her leaue at* Marye
her Doughter, commendynge her to the mercye of God,
*withe muche Motherlye admonytions for her to praƈtice
and haue in remembraunce after her dayes.*

¶ *Caput* 14.

"ITHE Deathe his Bedyll of ymbecylitee
Hathe fent to fomen me oute of this life,
To ende the courfe of this fragilytee
As is of Deathe the olde prerogatife,
Notwitheftandynge thoughe Nature makethe ftrife,
I wyll yeat nowe, emongeft other all,
Take leaue of *Mary* my Doughter fpeciall.

" O *Mary* mayden, by lyneall defcent
Spronge of the frefche and fweete Rofe rubycounde,
In florifchinge yeares, when hee was content
Withe the Pomegarnet on ftawlke to bee fownde,
Till ferpentyne fhakynge loafed the grounde,
Dyfceauerynge vs muche myferablye,
Wheare thorowe thowe art in heauynes drounde,
Yeat Jefu *thee faue of His great mercye !*

[*f.* 51.] " Of the haue I had greate comforte and joye
Hoapinge the fruyte of thy pofterytee,
Whiche Frayletee hathe wrought wrongely to annoye,
By meanys of flyckeringe Carnalytee,
Seeamynge as fugered fuauytee,
Mengeled withe poyfon, and lifte not efpye,
Greatlye makynge to thy calamytee;
Yeat Jefu *faue thee of His great mercy !*

" Sithe wycked woorkynge, muche colorably,
From that was thy dwe hathe fhyfted the owte,
Wrongely entreatynge, as truthe can teftifye,
By fundry compafinges fetchinge abowte,
Of thee (my deareft) I ftande in great dowbte,
Thoughe Childe for Parent ought not myfcarye :
So is Inyquytee nowe wexed ftowte ;
Yeat Jefu *faue thee of His great mercye !*

" Thowe, that wafte goaten in facred weddelock,
Art foarted nowe as illegitymat,
To the great fclaunder of thy worthye ftocke
Whiche on my parte was neauer viciat ;

Suche wayes this worlde dothe falſely imytat,
To the vndoinge of many á partye ;
But ſclaunderers God dothe excommunycat,
Who ſaue and keepe thee of His great mercye !

" Howe eauer contrary this worlde dothe frame,
His bloyſterous blaſtes behouethe to ſuſteyne ;
Heauynly rewarde enſuethe the ſame,
Who ſo for Truthes ſake refuſethe no payne,
Whiche Truthe in fyne no Falſehod may ſtayne ;
Withe patience thearfore, O Doughter *Mary,*
Arme thee alwayes, and Chriſte thy ſouereigne
Shall ſaue and keepe thee of His greate mercye.

" For all vnkyndenes that happen the ſhall,   [ſ. 51ᵇ.]
Vnto thy Father ſhewe due obedyence ;
As hee ſhall aſſigne thee, to riſe other fall,
Content thearwithe thyne inwarde conſcyence ;
So maiſte thoue haue of his beneuolence,
If Pytee or Mercye in hym dothe oughtes lye ;
In nowiſe to any woorke thoue offenſe,
And Chriſte *ſhall graunte thee of His mercye.*

" If eauer God ſhall thee ſet in Eſtate
(As, what Hee will dooe, noman can defyne),
Vnto thy Countrey bee neauer ingrate,
To dooe them comforte thy harte let inclyne ;
So ſhalte thoue ſhewe thee true Doughter of myne,
For I them loued withe all feruencye,
And they lykewiſe mee in perfecte true lyne ;
For whiche Chriſte Jeſus *graunte them His mercye !*

" The pooare (to thy poure) releeaue and ſuſteyne,
Thearby thoue ſhalte heere great goodnes purchace ;
Afwell of the pooare as the riche be fayne,
Specially tenderinge their neadful cafe ;
Euermore mercy withe pytee embrace,
So ſhalte thoue laye vpp thy treaſure on hye,
And ſhalte abounde withe Goddys ſpeciall grace,
Who ſaue and keepe thee of His great mercye !

" Bee meeke and lowlye in harte and in looke,
Beare thee not bolde of thy nobylitee ;
Bufye thy felfe in Goddys dyuyne Booke,
Whiche teachethe the rulys of pure humylitee ;
Bewares the wayes of falfe fragilitee,
Vfe faſtynge and prayinge for beſt remeadye ;
So ſhalte thoue trulye withe all facylitee
Purcheſſe of God *His fauour and mercye.*

[ƒ. 52.] " So ſhalte thoue bee in His ſpeciall fauour ;
So ſhalte thoue of man the daungers efcape ;
So ſhalte thoue purcheſſe heauyn for thy labour ;
So ſhall the Higheſt in thy behaulfe ſhape,
And thee ſaufelye ſheelde from all maner rape ;
If thoue to ſerue Hym wylte truly applye,
Hee withe thye enemyes will tryfle nor iape,
For that Hee bearethe thee His louynge mercye.

" Attende (O Doughter !) vnto my doctryne ;
Some (I well hoape) will thee thearof inſtructe
Thoughe I not fee thee withe corporall iyene,
Yeat owte of my harte thoue art not educte ;

As mee (thy Mother) bee thoue not illuᵉte,
God it forbeade! I pray Hym hartelye!
After His pleaſure His grace thee conduᵉte,
And ſaufely keepe thee of His great mercye!

" And nowe farewell, deeare Doughter *Mary!*
Farewell pooare Orphan, as ſeemethe vnto mee!
Farewell, whome fayne I wolde not myſcary!
Farewell, of forſe I neadys muſte forgoe thee!
Farewell in Hym that is bothe One and Three!
Farewell, ſrom ſeeinge thee withe mortall iye!
Farewell, nowe flowringe in virgynytee!
Jeſu *thee preſerue of His great mercye!*

" To take oure leaues each one of other,
Firſte thoue of mee (as Nature wolde ſo),
And I of thee, thy ſickely Mother,
That oute of this worlde is ready to goe,
It is prohybite, to my mortall woe;
Thoughe no diſcretion declarethe cauſe whie,
Indignation thee keepethe mee froe;
Yeat Jeſu *ſaue thee of His great mercye!*

" Halas! that I myght thee yeat onſe beholde   [*f.* 52ᵇ.]
Before that Deathe ſhall bereaue mee my ſight,
To bleſſe thee withe hande, thoughe earthelye and colde,
As ynwardely ſeruethe my appetyte,
To whiche (as I wolde) I am impedyte;
Thoughe reaſon it weare, the worlde dothe deny;
Goddys will bee fulfilled, as yt is right,
Who ſaue and keepe thee of His great mercy!

" The God of *Abraham* His bleſſinge geeue thee !
The God of *Iſahac* graunte thee the ſame !
The God of *Jacob* thy ſuccurrer bee,
Thee to defende from all worldely ſhame,
And to ſee proſper, to glory of His name,
This worlde (for His ſake) clearly to defye,
After His pleaſure thy lyuynge to frame,
Who ſaue and keepe thee of His great mercy !

" And as olde *Abraham* dyd *Iſahac* bleſſe,
And *Iſahac Jacob*, called *Iſraell,*
And *Jacob Joſeph*, Geneſis dothe expreſſe,
In awe of Goddys lawe they truly to dwell,
And other Bleſſed, as Scrypture dothe tell,
So bleſſe I thee withe bleſſinge ſemblably,
In name of the myghtye *Emanuel,*
Who ſaue and keepe thee of His great mercye !

" What bleſſynges more to Mother dothe pertayne,
If thouſandys they bee, on thee they alight,
Withe bleſſinge of God euer to remayne,
On thee (my Doughter) thee well to acquyte,
Of all falſe enemyes to voyde the deſpyte,
To pleaſure of God moſte ſpecyallye,
In his cauſe (as man) manfully to fight,
Who ſaue and keepe thee of His great mercy !

[*f.* 53.]   " Thus byd I thee (Doughter) for euer farewell !
Farewell ! farewell ! in ſorowes ſurely pight !
Farewell I bydde thee ! Deathes panges dothe compell,
The daye dyſpayrethe, faſte drawethe vnto nyght,

Yeat after dymme clowdys I hoape the Sunne bright,
That ſhynethe vnclypſed eauerlaſtingely ;
Hee make thee partyner of that heauynlye light
That is . . . . the Father of endeles mercye !   [*A word
                                                          eraſed.*]

" To Whome I beſeache thee, (*Mary*) deere Chylde,
To praye that Hee pleaſe my ſynnes to forgeeue,
That from His Preſence I bee not exilde,
Throughe tendre pytee that maye Hym ſo meeue,
For that in Hym I dooe only beleeue
And eauer haue doone, Hee wotethe it trulye ;
Thus, fayntynge for breathe, I neadys muſte bee breeue,
Commendinge the (Doughter) *to Goddys mercye !* "

¶ *Of* Gryſildis *godly departynge this life ; Her trobles
heere ended, euerlaſtinge reſt enſued. Wheare awe of
God is not, what myſeryes enſuethe. An Elucidation
vpon this texte,* In Domo Patris mei Manſiones multæ
ſunt, *approuynge, whoe ſeruethe highelye (as did this
Gryſilde) is of* God *highely rewarded.*

¶ *Caput* 15.

FF this noble woman the day beinge come
Her corps to rendre to wheare it firſte ſpronge,
As was ſo ordayned by Goddis dyuyne dome,
Leſte in departinge the ſame myght haue
wronge,
After ſhee had in ſicknes traueylde longe,
Shee humblye beſought, withe hartys compunētion,
To haue (as was dwe) the *Extreme Vnētion.*

Q

[ʃ. 53ᵇ.] Whearwithe munyted, in true Chriſtian ſorte,
Agaynſte tranſgreſſion of the ſenſes fyue,
So ſealynge then vpp eache highe waye or porte,
The lyttle life leſte began as to ſtryue,
As thoughe againſte Deathe it fayne wolde reuyue,
But thearby brought in ſuperation,
She of her ſpirite gaue expiration.

So weare her trobles heere brought to an ende,
After of ſundrye thexpeſtation,
Vnto that purpoſe whiche longe did attende,
Thoughe, cheiflye of all, to her conſolation,
For reſte was to her after trybulation ;
None otherwiſe I can in harte eſteeme
But, ſufferinge for right, to weare the dyadeeme.

And thoughe ſhee heere (in this life tranſitorye)
Weare of her honour and kyngedome ſhut owte,
Into a kyngedome of farre more glorye
Shee was receaued, I haue no myſdoubte ;
So, for her, her heauynly Kynge brought abowte,
Whiche neauer faylethe all thoſe Hym ſeruynge,
That well ys to ſerue ſo noble á Kynge ;

Whome all her lifetyme ſhe truly obeyde,
And ſerued withe all her harte cowlde deuiſe,
As (partelye) heerein wee haue of her ſaide,
That ſo to credyte ynoughe may ſuffice ;
What more then needethe to tell á tale twice ?
Shee nowe departed (as earſte wee haue tolde),
So ended heere her trobles manyfolde.

So was the alterynge, by many á daye,
Nowe at á poynéte, tochynge the former cafe ;
Thoughe Newe vpon Newe theare followed nonaye,
As neauer the like in fo little fpace,
And no lyttle fpace contynued the race,
For twentye yearys full, it day by day wrought
Till it had (almofte) brought all vnto nought.

Wheare dwe awe of God is feene negleéted,
Wheare wycked alfo dothe predomynat,
Wheare throughe falfe *Cupyde* the Royalme is infeéted,
Wheare meanys may none his foly mytigate,
Wheare the Holye men dothe contamynat,
Wheare libertee frayle is not refrayned,
Theare is the Countrey muche to bee wayled ;

Theare needys mufte reigne Goddys indignation ;
Wheare that fo dothe, this fequele mufte enfue,
Of His meere Grace clean depryuation ;
Depryued thearof, adieu all vertue,
In obduracye for to contynue,
So followeinge oure owne fragilytee,
As thoughe for fynne no punyfchment fholde bee.

Suche daungerous tyme was certaynlye feene
By alterations, as is áforefayde,
In the later dayes of this noble Queene,
Whearby vertue was vtterlye decayde,
Excepte in á fewe whiche God (by grace) ftayde,
As this goode *Gryfilde* fpecially one,
Owte of this life to His mercy nowe gone.

[*f.* 54ᵇ.] Somuche wee haue not of that goode woman
Mentioned heere to her commendation,
But lyuynge are manye that farre better can
Put her dooynges in commemoration,
To Goddys moſte worthie and highe veneration,
For that His Grace was her ſpeciall guyde
In vertuous patience to cauſe her abyde ;

To Whome, in   arte of recompenſation,
Beſydis her ſeruyce in this life mundayne,
As freendys by muche freendely ſalutation
Salutethe their freendys with giftes heere terrayne
At Newe yearys tyde, in frendeſhippe to remayne,
Shee to her Freende that beſte for her cowlde ſhifte,
Yealded her ſowle for her Newe yearys gifte.

For on Newe yearys eue (as I was inſtructed)
Shee yealded her gohoſte to her Redeamer,
And vnto His palace it was conducted,
By ſignes noleſſe, dyinge whoe had ſeene her,
Withe vertue floriſcheinge, no lawrer greener,
To thacceptation of her heauynly Lorde ;
To that He bought her ſhee was thearfore reſtorde,

And ſet in place (as well wee maye ſuppoſe)
Of heauynly blyſſe, moſte glorouſly ſhynynge,
For Chriſte in His Fathers howſe dothe diſcloſe
To bee Manſyons manye, of His deuyſinge,
Accordinge to heere the partyes merytinge ;
Then maye be ſaide, the gloryous in life
Of gloryous place to haue prerogatiſe.

As the mofte excellent *Virgyn Marye*
Dyd heere excell in vertue foueraigne,
So in the celeftiall fanctuarye
Her feate tranfcendethe all creatures certaigne ;
Of her fo to holde it is not in vayne,
For the Lorde theare (her Sunne and Iffue)
As mother nexte Hym ought her to indue.

*[f. 55.]
Exaltata eft
fuper choros
Angelorum,ca-
nit Ecclefia.*

Of *John* the *Baptifte* maye alfo be thought,
For that Chrifte (Hym felfe) hym praifed fo highlye,
Thearto aecordynge in place to bee brought ;
None higher then hee of humayne progenye,
Excepte (beforefaide) oure bleffed Ladye ;
In all comparafons of vertue and grace
Shee of all creatures mufte haue the cheif place.

*Inter natos
mulierum non
furrexit major
Joanne Bap-
tifta.* [St.
Luke vii. 28]

John the *Euangelifte*, a pure Virgyn,
That Chrifte permytted to fleepe on His brefte,
Whiche, neauer corrupted withe flefchely fynne,
Mufte neadys in heauyn haue highe enterefte ;
That life (of all lyues) is theare alowed befte,
For they whoe theare can bee approued fo
Followe the *Lambe* wheare eauer Hee dothe goe.

*Supra pectus
Domini in Cena
recubuit.*

[Rev. xiv. 4.]

Holy Saincte *Pawle* that, paffinge other all,
Labored in preachynge of Chryftes gofpell,
Hathe he not (trowe yee) a farre higher ftall
Then other that not fomuche dyd trauell ?
As lobour (*fic*) mountethe, rewarde dothe excell ;
Whoe fowethe muche, abundantly fhall mowe,
And hee but lyttle that lyttle dothe fowe.

*Ego plus omni-
bus laboraui.*
[1 Cor. xv. 10.]

[2 Cor. ix. 6.]

[ƒ 55ᵇ·] The holy martyrs *Laurénce* and *Vincent*,
Stephyn and *Dyonyſe*, withe other ſuche mo,
Endurynge for Chriſte moſt greuous torment,
Eauyn tyll the Tortours themſelfes liſte bydde, Whoe!
Shall other (in joye) ſo paſſyngelye go
That quyetlye endethe, thoughe Chriſtyanlye?
No; theare is certayne indyfferencye.

The *Theeif* that henge on Chryſtys right ſyde,
Whiche moſte his lyfe tyme myſerablye ledde,
Whome Chriſte (His mercye to haue that tyme tryde)
Tooke to His joyes after hee was dedde,
And was of the ſame ſuffyciently ſpedde,
Yeat to bee weyed (as I dooe take ytt)
His meryte withe *Pawle*, noman may make ytt.

But, vndreſtande yee, in this to conclude,
The mynde of ſome ſomewhat to ſatysfye :
Aboue the celeſtiall Beatytude
Theare is no maner of controuerſye,
But peace abydynge perpetuallye,
Withe ſuche charytable eſtabliſchment
That but perfecte vnytee dothe theare frequent.

Theare the Higheſt withe Meaneſt compared,
Eyther of other hathe this opynyon,
So equalye theare to bee rewarded
That but to them is one Fruytion,
And ſo it is in this condition,
For the Viſyon of the Deytee
Is theare theyr full and whoale felycitee.

That hathe the Higheſt, that hathe the Meaneſt,   [*ſ.* 56.]
That is euyn all, and all is yn that;
But whoe in this life hathe lyued cleaneſt,
In portion paſſinge dothe ſo contemplat;
Then is this *Gryſilde* in place ſituat,
Not withe the ſlackeſt, that after noone çame,   [St. Matt. xx.]
But withe the earlieſt; her life ſhewethe the ſame.

For euyn from the tyme ſhe had diſcretion
Vnto the ſeaſon her life dyd expyre,
She (trulye) ſerued withe full affeċtion;
Thearto accordynge, ſhe hathe for her hyre;
Not as the *Murmurer* ſhe dyd requyre,   [St. Matt.
But, hoapynge rewarde of endeleſſe ſolace,   xx. 11.]
Shee her commended vnto her Lordys grace.

As of this woman oure verduyte is ſuche,
So of all other that lyued as dyd ſhee;
Whis [*whois*] traueyle is great, his rewarde ys muche,
Such is the goodnes of Goddys maieſtee;
On which preaſumynge, thereby judge wee
This godly *Gryſilde* nowe, after her peyne,
With Hym in reſte eauerlaſtynge to reigne.

¶ *So ſoone as Walter had vndreſtandynge by certayne report*
howe Gryſildys *life was henſe ſeperat, he commaunded*
at Peter Burrowe *to haue her buried, muche honprablye ;*
Of the maner thearof.   Shee lyuynge as ſhe dyd (holely)
cowlde not but haue goode. endinge, thoughe not ſo of the
praue ſorte ; Her Corone heere taken from her, an euer-
laſtinge was reſtored.

¶ Cap. 16.

[ƒ. 56.ᵇ]   S *Walter* had perfecte vndreſtandynge
Griſilde from this life to bee ſeperat,
It moued his harte by inwarde wandringe
To haue her worthelye intumulat,
Accordynge to her honorable eſtate,
Commaundynge his Offycers (by reporte)
That it weare doone in conuenyent forte.

Ferdre, his wyll was her buryall to bee
In the See Churche of *Peterborowe ;*
After whois pleaſure thither brought was ſhee,
The Ordre as howe I lyſte not tell thorowe,
But, paſſinge ouer many á forowe,
Feelde and leaſues, withe medowys freſche and greene,
In ordynary ſorte, as hathe beene ſeene.

Theare weare in ordre the Offycers ſett,
As in thobſequye of Pryncelye eſtate,
Bothe Trumpetours and Herawtes, theare they mett,
To dooe accordynge as ſyttethe the rate,
Withe Ladyes lamentynge her mortall fate,
Whiche, thoughe it bee moſte naturall and ſure,
Suche (yeat of freendys) is the cuſtome and vre.

Brought to the place, muche honorablye,
The deadde cadauer of this noble Queene,
Suche hearffe of waxe, wrought curyouflye,
Was theare vpp fett as feelde hathe earfte bee feene ;
The fame deadde bodye amyddys theare betweene,
Withe fundrye ryche clothes vpon the hearffe layde
For purpofe whiche heere not neadethe to bee fayde.

Executor cheeife of this obfequye   [*f.* 57.]
Was the Busfhoppe mentioned before,
Affifted by twoe, withe all dyligencye,
Of the fame ordre, witheoute anye more,
Saue Abbottes and other Religious great ftore,
Synginge and fayinge, as thearto was dwe,
Dirige and Maffe, while tyme dyd contynue.

In tyme of whiche, the Herawtes theare prefent,
At eauery Pfalme and Leffon ended,
From the faide hearffe they tooke as they went
Some certaigne thynge, for caufe pretended,
Signyfyinge, the honor God lended
Vnto that ladye, in fuche riche araye,
Was (fynallye) heere from her take awaye.

At Offerynge tyme the trumpettes dyd blowe
Eauerye Eftate to take his degree,
By fownde of whiche they perfectlye did knowe
Who firfte, whoe feconde, and who lafte to bee ;
Whiche fight, thoughe pyteful it was to fee,
Yeat the ordre was muche honorable,
Farre paffynge texpreffe then I am hable.

R

The Maſſe completed to the Buryall,
Withe lightes and torches wondreful manye,
And numbre of people bothe great and ſmall,
Preparynge was the bodye to carye
Vnto the place wheare it ſhoulde tarye ;
Proceadinge furthe in honorable wiſe,
Hundreadys theare followynge withe watrye iyes.

[ſ. 57ᵇ.]   And in that ſaide churche, all on the northe ſyde,
At thende of this right ſolempne funerall,
Her corps (in cophyn) they did it theare hyde,
Lowe in the earthe, to reſte perpetuall,
Wheare, in tokne of this exchaunge mortall,
The Offycers all, withe muche heauye chere,
Their roddys breakynge caſte in her ſepulchere.

So was this noble and godlye woman,
(After the courſe of this mortalytee)
Layde in the colde earthe of whiche ſhee began,
Notwitheſtandynge her highe nobylytee ;
For whome was dealte vnto the Pouertee
Neare to the ſumme of one hundred pownde,
The daye of renderynge her corps to the grounde.

Of whiche her deathe and lyfes disjunction
All goode folke joyed, in Goddys ſo ordynaunce ;
For dyinge heere in true compunction
Is ſigne moſte ſure of heauyns inherytaunce,
As dyd this woman by goode aſſuraunce,
Whoe all her lyfe dayes was to God pleaſinge,
Wheaffore ſhee cowlde not but haue goode endinge.

But, contrary wife, whoe lyuethe at ryat
Flefchely and beaftely, as leadethe blynde lufte,
Reauynge and ragynge, all owte of quyat,
As, what the flefche wyll, neadys haue yt hee mufte,
Of fuche the fauegarde I haue in myftrufte ;
For Synne accuftomynge, Experyence dothe tell,
In fyne of the fame wyll haue á great fmell.

Thoughe " *inter Pontem et Fontem* " (ys fayde)   [*f.* 5ᵇ.]
One certaigne theare was that fownde meede of grace,
In hoape of the like, in mynde bee yt wayde,
Let no man fynne, Goddys mercye to purchace,
But vertue tenure while heere is lent fpace ;
Of fuche, whois life is merytoryous,
In fight of God the deathe is preacyous.

Of fynners not fo, fetteled in malice,
But is mofte odyous in Goddys dyuyne fight,
Withe contrarye rewarde myxte is their chalice,
Fyre and fulphur to the fynner of right ;
The godly joyned to heauynlye delyte ;
Whiche dyuerfiteis, wifelye adnoted,
Geauethe occafion fynne to bee lothed.

As dyd this noble and godlye *Gryfilde*,
All her whoale life tyme heere fynne forfakynge ;
What was to Goddys pleafure fhe gladly fulfilde,
The pooare and neadye greatlye comfortynge ;
Whearfore Hee wolde her to haue refortynge
Vnto His heauynlye habytation,
To haue perdurable Coronation.

Thoughe heere her Córóne was her depryued,
The other fhoulde neauer haue defe&ion ;
So had the Higheft for her contryued
In His æterne præfcient Ele&ion,
To Whome althyngis are in fubje&ion,
Bothe heauynly, earthely, and lowe in the Hell,
Wythe hartys of all Kyngis to wyll and compell ;

[*f.* 58ᵇ.]   And dyd (nodowbte) for her, His true feruaunte,
At ende of this relynquyfcheinge her life,
Woorke in *Walter* that hee fhoulde neadys graunte
To haue her buryed like to Pryncys wife ;
Suche was (thorowe Hym) her prerogatife,
Receauynge her fowle to His heauynlye blyffe,
Whois grace dyre&e vs the waye not to myffe.

¶ *The maner (muche parte) of the dolefull complaynte and
lamentation of the mofte gratious and vertuous Pryncęffe
Marye for the departure of her noble mother goode
Gryfilidis, fhe beyngé (thoughe abfent) the Mooarner cheeif
inthobfequye of her Funerall; and of her fylyall commendynge her vnto theauerlaftinge mercy of almyghtie God.*

¶ *Caput* 17.

N funerye of this áforefaide woman
Is to bee had in confyderation
Who was cheeif *Mooarner* to be compted than,
Of all the thronge and congregation ;
For, to expreffe in breeue narration,
It was her deere Doughter *Marye* (by name)
Thoughe abfent fhe weare, and kepte from the fame ;

She was cheeif *Mooarner*, it well maye bee faide,
All other to her weare but as countrefettes ;
She, heearynge her Mother vndre booarde laide,
In to her clofett demurelye fhee gettes,
Her cheeakes all withe tearys fhe ruthefully wettes,
Kneealynge á downe in contemplation,
. Lamentynge her Mother vndre this fafhion :—

" O heauynly Father and Kynge celeftiall,   [*f.* 59.]
Lorde of all Lordys, Thy tytle ys fo,
To Whorîe fpecyall obeyfaunce dothe fall,
Thy ordynaunce dyuyne no man may parte fro,
All one to conuynce, in feawe as in mo,
My Mother henfe rapte from this worldys vifion
To wheare Thowe pleafifte to haue her to go,
Thowe graunte her, (Lorde), *Thy heauynly fruition !*

" Her to commaunde to demore or departe
Thy office it is, none may Thee refifte,
Her Thowe heere madifte by Thy dyuyne arte,
And woldifte to tarrye fo longe as Thowe lifte,
Tyll nowe her life threade Thowe lifte to vntwifte
(As in all flefche for mannys punytion)
Whoe (naturally) of mee is fore myfte,
Yeat graunte her, (Lorde), *Thy heauynly fruition !*

" From tyme fhe was firfte in wombe conceaued
Vnto the daye of her dyffeauerynge,
Of her the tradynge Thowe neauer leaued,
But wafte her Guyde, her lyfe aye orderynge,

And as Thowe woldiſte ſhe was conformynge ;
Thy grace (from evyll) was her munytion ;
As Thowe haſte ſo to her beene tenderynge,
So graunte her, (Lorde), *Thy heauynly fruition!*

" After, (in proceſſe), as Thowe liſte vouchefaue,
Thowe hyther conueidſte her, at Thy pleaſure,
Wheare to the ſame ſhee dyd her behaue,
Thoughe ſorowes ſought her farre oute of meaſure,

[*f.* 59ᵇ.] Throughe whiche, withe Thee, ſhe heaped vpp treaſure,
For that ſhe loued no ſedytion
But ſerued Thee trulye, as ſhee had leaſure ;
Whearfore, Thowe graunte her Thy heauynly fruition!

" And nowe Thowe pleaſiſte her trobles to fyne
Heere in this ſtate of myſerye and care,
And ſhee to repayre wheare Thowe liſte aſſigne,
Wheare Thy ſeruauntes and true beleauers are,
As thorowe Thy mercye I well credyte dare,
Bycauſe ſhee ended withe true contrytion ;
For Thowe to all ſuche digne Judgement doiſte ſpare,
And grauntiſte freelye Thy heauynlye fruition.

" So is my hoape in Thye benygne mercye
That her Thowe haſte take to Thy heauynly reſte,
Thee eauermore to praiſe and magnyfie,
As Thowe canſte ordayne thynges all for the beſte ;
And, bleſſed Lorde, graunte this humble requeſte,
That I maye bee of like condytion,
After her life my life to ſee dreſte,
Withe her to haue Thy heauynly fruition!

" Of whome (my Mother and Educatrice)
Callynge to mynde her conuerſation,
I cannot but in moſte dolorous wiſe
Fall into thoughtfull lamentation,
To myſſe her motherly conſolation ;
But, ſithe it cummethe of Goddys prouyſion,
I can but wiſche her ſowlys ſaluation,
To haue withe Hym of His fruytion.

" Thowe parted this life, O meeke Mother myne !   [/. 60.]
The louyngiſte that eauer to chylde myght bee,
What ſhall I dooe but this worldys joyes reſigne,
And daylye praye God to fetche mee to thee ?
In tyme thowe lyuydſte I felte aduerſytee,
And muche more hangethe of dyſpoſition ;
God I beſeache His pleaſure dooe withe mee,
And thee to graunte His heauynlye fruytion.

" While life in mee laſtethe I ſhall not forget
To mee (thy childe) thy motherly tendrenes ;
Of fylyall duetye I am ſo in debte
By what meanys I maye the ſame to expreſſe,
Thoughe not (as to ſaye) in ſignes of heauynes,
But hartye prayer and meeke petytion,
That God (of His ineffable goodnes)
Will graunte to thee His heauynly fruytion.

" And, as for thee (daylye) I ſhall ſo praye
Whyle in this life I haue contynuaunce,
So praye thowe for mee, I truſte thowe ſo maye,
Teſcape of this worlde the falſe conueyaunce,

Withe what els enemyes woorkethe me annoyaunce
By falſe and ſathanyke ſedytion,
The heauynly Kynge to ſhewe His puyſaunce,
And thee to graunte His heauynly fruytion.

" What is of this life the pómpous eſtate
But (as to ſaye) á burdayne ponderous,
Witht [*ſic*] ſundrye chargys that dothe onerat
Of ſtreyte accompte to Chriſte moſte gloryous,
[ſ. 60ᵇ.] Excepte true bearynge, whiche is meruelous,
Only graunted throughe Goddys prouyſion ;
So ys oure nature ſownde contraryous,
That voydethe vs ofte from His fruition.

" But thowe (my Mother), nowe voyded this light,
So eauenlye lyuydiſte in thy vocation
Towardys heere all ſortys, the Goode can recyte,
That ſoone was made thy computation,
So ſeruethe my imagynation ;
So godly was thy dyſpoſition,
All vyce thowe puttidſte in ſequeſtration,
Whearfore thowe haſte of Goddys fruition.

" So is my hoape in God my Creator,
So ys to Hym my quotydyan requeſte,
So ys the woonte of Hym (the Grace Dator)
All ſuche to receaue in His heauynlye reſte,
Speciallye thoſe for right heere ſuppreſte,
Meekelye ſufferynge this worldys punytion ;
Of whiche wronged ſorte thowe maiſte bee confeſte,
And numbred to haue of His fruytion.

" To whome thy fowle, of His Creation,
Withe all fubmyffion I meekelye commende,
Befeachynge His myghtye Domynation
From this worldys malice mee faufe to defende,
Whiche fuethe the wayes that lowe dothe defcende
Vnto the lake of fowle Perdytion,
But thee and mee, that otherwife entende,
To haue (for eauer) of His fruytion."

Suche was this Maydyns meditation   [*J.* 61.]
For her dȩeare Mother, to her mofte louynge,
Withe harte fore plunged in perturbation
Throughe fundrye ftormys her ftrongely prouynge,
Yeat fhee all conftante, ftandynge vnmouynge,
Specially hoapynge in Goddys tuytion,
As mofte neadfull to her was behouynge,
To wynne the fruyte of His fruytion.

The Mother departed this mundayne life,
Thȩ Doughter remaynynge, compafte with care,
The wicked withe her at contynuall ftrife,
The enuyous ferpent to tempte her fo dare,
The feruauntys of hym the like dyd not fpare ;
As abjeɛte, fhee lyued in muche derifion ;
So leaue I her, all voyde of hartys welfare,
But only in hoape of Goddys fruytion.

¶ *A conferrynge betweene the* firſte Walter *and the* Seconde,
The firſte Gryſilde *and the* Seconde, *approuynge the*
Seconde Gryſilde *of farre more worthy eſtymation then
the* Firſte, *alſo her* Maryage *to be moſte lawful ; Of whis*
Iſſue *heauyn and earthe reioyced.*

¶ *Cap.* 18.

O clokedlye vndre darke couerture
We haue not walked in this Hiſtorye,
But that the readers may vndreſtande ſure
The meane of oure mentioned memorye,
Not fygured as by Alligorye,
But this ſayde *Gryſilde*, playnlye to defyne,
Is playnlye ment the goode Queene *Catharyne.*

[ſ. 61ᵇ.] *Walter* (her huſbonde) kynge *Henry* the Eight,
A man muche noble in pryncely corage,
Yeat in this mateir, importynge great weight,
He was wronge leadde and wandred at outrage,
(As may well bee thought, throughe louys dotage,
Loue leacherous, inconſtante and ſycle,
Whiche in the frayle dothe ſtooare and muche prycle.)

Whye wee compare *Catharyne* to *Gryſilde,*
Henry to *Walter*, as ſhewthe evydence,
For that in thys Newe is mateir dyſtilde
As in the Olde, conſyderinge pretence,
Withe farre paſſinge vehementer offenſe
Of *Henryes* party to *Catharyne* was dooe,
Then eauer *Walter* ſhewde *Gryſilde* vntooe.

Fyrſte, *Walter*, á man of highe nobylitee,
To *Gryſilde* (farre baſe) auouched to knytt,
Whoe ſhewed her tatcheſſe of inſtabylitee
When from her feloweſhippe he neadys wolde flytt,
Her childred hee made as buryed in pytte;
Relynquiſchinge her, hee tooke her ágayne,
And in this all whoale hee dyd hym but fayne.

This alter *Walter*, not joyned in baſe,
But in all honour machte with his equall,
Relynquiſchinge her, hee had not the grace
Her as to ſett in her priſtynat ſtall,
But earneſtely wrought her harte to appall,
Witheoute all maner reconciliation,
Tyll Deathe (in her ſorte) made ſeperation.

Howemuche as *Gryſilde* the Firſte (as wee meane)   [*f.* 61.]
Was iſſued of meane and lowe progeniture,
Somuche the eaſyer ſhee myght faſchyon cleane
The ſturdye dooynges of *Walter* tendure;
Lowe, lowe to bee brought, not peſtrethe Nature,
Lowe eaſyer maye aduerſitee ſuſteyne
Then Highe in myſerye lowe to compleyne.

Walter the Firſte his iſſue not hated,
But foſtred the ſame muche honorablye;
Thother *Walter* his iſſue abated
That was of hym iſſued moſte lawfullye;
So was betweene them great dyfferencye;
The Firſte muche kynde, thoughe he diſſymuled,
Thother vnkynde, as maye bee lykened.

Thus *Walter* withe *Walter* hathe lykelynes,
For vnto their wyues commyttynge offenſe ;
And *Gryfilde* to *Gryfilde* lykewiſe to geſſe,
For their meeke ſufferynge and patience ;
But muche more is to haue preamynence
The *Seconde Gryfilde*, by goode authorytee,
Then the *Fyrſte*, as reaſon ſeemethe to mee.

For of her great Patience theare is nodowbte,
Her faƈtes in preſent remembraunce dothe reigne ;
The *Firſte* howe her dooynges weare brought abowte,
To vs in theis dayes they are vncertayne ;
Many imagyne that *Petrarke* dyd but fayne ;
Howe muche the *Seconde* is true, that yee haue herde,
Somuche before *thother* ſhee is too bee preferde.

[ʄ. 62ᵇ.]   And ſithe that Ethnykes accuſtomed (of olde)
The famous aƈtys of their noble women
In ſorte of Hiſtoryes to haue enrolde,
As Hiſtoryographys ſawe worthye to penne,
Howe muche in thois oure later dayes, then,
Of ſuche noble woman as oure *Gryfilde* was
To haue her hiſtorye brought vnto paſſe.

In whiche I haue ſayde as my knowledge leadethe,
And as of oother I haue beene inſtruƈted ;
If anye heere after that this ſame readethe,
By ferdre knowledge beeynge conduƈted,
Shall ſeeme the dwe I haue ouerfluƈted,
Let hym take yt in reformation,
That more maye ſerue to acceptation.

I weare muche lothe of highe other lowe
To bee fownde fawtye yn my compryſinge,
But farre loather opynyon wronge to growe,
When I am gone, by this my ſaide wrytinge ;
Rather I had myſſe forme of endytinge
(As to ſaye, meeaters true obſeruation)
Then to leaue this in varyation.

Theare are that muche more can ſaye in this
Bycawſe muche more they ſawe in practice,
Whiche withe this ladye *Gryſylidis*
Weare conuerſante and dyd her ſeruyce,
But to my purpoſe this dothe ſuffice,
Withe ſomewhat ferdre comprobation
That wrongefull was her ſeperation.

The tradynge totall of this compryſement　　　　[*ſ. 63.*]
Perſwadethe of wrongis to *Gryſilidis*,
Approued by ſequele moſte euydent ;
As, to the purpoſe receaued nowe this,
To her was argued, ſhe was ſterilis,
Alſo wife to *Walters* brother dedde,
Whearfore ſhe was to bee repudied.

To whiche objection concurryngely take,
That ſhee reiected and newe receaued,
The beſte that myght vnto the purpoſe make,
Whearby iſſue myght bee conceaued,
From one to fyue to bee alleaued ;
And yeat (in fyne) whoe liſte to vndreſtande
To *Gryſildys* ſeade the State was brought to hande.

If wronge had bee their copulation,
God wolde of wronge (Whiche is endleſſe Right)
Not ſo haue ſet in eſtymation
That wrongefull weare in His heauynly ſight ;
But, beeinge rightfull, by His dyuyne myght,
Hathe *Gryſildys* ſeade in honor exalted,
Thoughe earſte (as baſe) yt farre á lowe halted.

At whois pryncelye Inthronization
(Muche meruouſly by God brought abowte)
The Heauynlye Spyrytes made Jubilation
As my conſcyence perſwadethe owte of dowbte,
For that His enemyes withe her beare no rowte,
Falſe Hereſyarkes, poyſonlye harted,
That earſte Goddys glorye had neare peruerted.

[ſ. 63ᵇ.] For, moſte certaynly, wheare wicked Sathan
Withe his tortuous wayes is eiected,
Purged and clenſed as God ordayne can,
And His dwe honor trulye erected,
Theare (credyblye) the Spirytes elected
(As in the conuerſion of ſynners to grace)
Takethe occaſion of heauynlye ſolace.

And, as the celeſtyall Hierarchies ſo
Of oure conuerſion reioyced ſuche wiſe,
So thowſande thowſande withe hundredfolde mo
Withe joyinges in God their hartys did ſuffice,
To ſee that was downe agayne to ariſe,
The Chriſtian Faythe withe Hereſye oppreſt,
As they had cawſe moſte certaynly earneſt.

Emonges all whiche, mofte fpeciallye of all,
Wee Englifche Men ought to rendre God thankes,
That vs Hee pleafed to grace agayne call,
Whiche weare as men cafte ouer the feaye bankes
Into the Carybdis of feendelye phalankes,
Withe them to gnafche in defperation
For oure from God falfe feperation.

For Faythe was heere (in maner) neare extyncte
Withe muche hydeous innouation,
The Badde agaynfte the Goode dyuyllifchly lynkte
By tomuche hatefull indignation ;
The pledge heere left to oure faluation
Of *Chryftys bodye* that bought vs from blame,
None heere fo hardye in right forte to name.

Whearfore to God bee fpeciall dwe prayfe,   [*f.* 64]
For that (of His mercye fuperabundaunte)
Hee pleafed for vs to woorke in fuche wayfe,
Thoughe wee to His lawes weare farre repugnaunte,
Whoe graunte vs nomore to bee inconftaunte,
For pleafe Hym wee cannot, the Scripture faithe,   [Heb xi. 6.]
Wee feaueringe from the Catholique faithe.

¶ Gryſilde, *departed to* God, *prayethe for vs, wee neeade
not to dowbte, thoughe ſome (of wronge opynyon) holdethe
the prayer of* Sayntes *to profite nowhyt ; à brobation
[ſic] to the contrary, and that* Englande *by the prayer
of the bleſſed aboue was (of late) reduced to the Chriſtian
Faithe àgayne (as wee maye well ſuppoſe) that weare gone
aſtraye.*

Caput 19.

*Gryſilde,reign-
ynge withe
God, dothe
praye for vs
is not to bee
doubted.*

WRE Chriſtian *Griſilde,* as ye haue herde tell,
Rendred to the grownde, as right ſo ſhall wee,
In mercy of God I leaue her to dwell,
Partyners withe her Who graunte vs to bee ;
Shee, joyinge the heauynlye felycitee,
For vs (her olde ſubjectes), I dare well ſaye,
In all oure trobles dothe inſtantlye praye ;

Thoughe myſerable men, inſanyat and groſe,
Seduced by Sathan, the Prynce of darkenes,
For Sayntes in glorye dothe wrongelye depoſe
Theye weeit not owre prayinges to them in diſtreſſe,
Nor oughtes can helpe to eaſe oure heauynes
By prayinge for vs to oure heauynlye Father ;
Whois errour to ceaſſe, theis prooues I gather :—

[f. 4ᵇ.] If only to God owre thoughtys inwardelye
(By prayer or els) bee perfectelye knowne,
And to none other His creatures on hye,
Then weare the ordynaunce quyte ouer throwne
Whiche in Chriſtys Churche of conſuetude is growne,
Howe the Angels and Sowlys in reſte aboue
Dothe impetrat God for ſynners behoue.

In Earthe, wee haue knowledge, by holye *Jeamys,*   [St. James v. 16.]
Howe muche dothe profyte the prayre of the Jufte ;
Then, they nowe regnynge aboue the funne beamys,
In farre higher fauour withe God wee graunte mufte,
For owte of fauour none can them theare thrufte,
The more in fauoure, the more profyte they maye,
As, to optayne what eauer they for praye.

And of the Lorde mofte renowmed (*fic*) and great,
(The highe, myghtye, and Creator of all),
This is alwayes the accuftomed feate,
His feruauntys heere that to Hym afcende fhall
In Heauyn to indwe withe grace more fpecyall ;
Then, if theyr prayer maye profite in this life,
In Heauyn they hathe farre more prerogatife.

If Angels (whiche are but creatures certayne)
Dothe knowe the fynners conuerfyon to grace,
Whiche conuerfion is yn the harte playne,
For fpeciall prooif, and not by the face,
Then, Saynctes maye the like, in femblable cafe,
Sithe God his Freendys lifte them fo nomynat,   [St. John xv. 15.]
And fhall in judgement withe Hym affociat.

The Angels, the Scripture dothe playnly declare,   [*f.* 65.]
Reioycethe farre more in one fynners amendement -   [St. Luke xv. 7.]
Then in great numbers that innoxious are
Whiche neaded not to bee come penytent,
And, like fo the Sayntes, by forme confequent
For that, as Angels, they creatures bee,
And dothe (withe them) pytee oure infirmytee.

T

If Dyuyllis oure euyl deadys and thoughtes contraryous*
Shall laye to oure chargis, not purged by peanaunce,
Then knowe they oure fawtes, by proofe notoryous;
Whye els dothe Scripture put yn remembraunce
Howe Sathan, that workethe vs all his vengeaunce,
In *Judas* harte entred, and wrought theare the waye
His Maifter (*Chriſte Jeſus*) to fell and betraye?

[Tobit xii, 12.] Of *Thobye* wee reade howe that *Raphael*
(Goddys Medycyne, by interpretation)
His prayers, made in his hartys fecreat cell,
To God of them hee made prefentation;
And, as of *Thoby* in fuche fayde faſchyon,
So oure goode Angels eache godlye entent
Of vs fulfilled to God dothe prefent.

Not that but fuche wayes He dothe them els weete,
(To Whois dyuyne iyes althynges are áperte),
But thorowe Charytee, that is fo fweete,
God wyll hys Spyrytes to woorke in couerte,
And alfo his Saynctes, of one lynked harte,
In like heauynlye loue that fo dothe excell,
To wyll and wyfche vs mofte earneſtlye well.

All whiche (their knowledge) in God they fee ytt,
As wee in the glaffe whoe ſtandethe behynde vs,
Thoughe the comparafon bee farre vnfytt;
So wyll Hee haue it, of His wyll gratious,
That as wee Worldelye in knoweledge curyous
Tranfcende the Brutall, by muche dyfference,
So vs the Heauynlye, by paffinge excellence.

* This ſtanza has been inferted in the margin as an addition.

Wee fee heere in earthe, faynête *Pawle* dothe expreffe, [f. 65ᵇ.]
As in a glaffe, or fhadowed myfterye; [1 Cor. xiii. 12.]
But theare, oure knowledge fhall have ful perfeêtnes,
Witheowte obumbraunce or other fallacye.
Thearfore I argue, as in this partye,
Owre imperfeêtion in this ftate mundayne
To what Saynêtes maye dooe it cannot attayne.

Then, fithe holye Churchê, heere mylytante nowe,
Receauethe and teachethe their prayers to preuayle,
What fhoulde wee otherwife then fo allowe
If wee withe *Peter* in his fhippe will fayle?
Whoe holdethe by her, hys holde cannot fayle:
Then holde I, this *Grifildis* prayer to profite,
As Cytizyns of God throughe heauynly meryte.

For, owte of the waye as wee weare late ftreyed,
I fyrmelye beleeue throughe prayer made abooue
Of Saynêtes withe immortalytee arayed,
(That fo brennethe in charytee and looue,
As, to my feemynge, fenfyblye dothe prooue)
Wee weare reuoked and called vnto grace
From rennynge hedelynge oure dampnable râce.

As after this maner imagyne I maye
Their prayers for vs to fpreadde in Goddys fight:—
" O Thowe cleare fhynynge euerlaftynge Daye,
Thowe God That art of goodnes ynfynyte,
In Whome confiftethe all whoale oure delyte,
Vouchefaufe Thyne Earys to oure prayers inclyne,
Profterned to fore Thy maieftee dyuyne!

[*f.* 66.] " On Englande, that fometyme (as was mofte dwe)
Had Thee in jufte feare and digne reuerence,
Vntyll Thyne Enemye, that Thee dothe purfue,
(Thenuyous Serpent, full of peftylence,)
Oppreft the fame throughe Herefyes pretence,
Extende Thy mercye, and dooe not refufe
Them to Thy feruyce agayne to reduce.

" Remembre (O Lorde!) of this heauynlye Porte
Howe manye thowfandys dothe oure mynyfterye
Vnto Thy majeftee, in owre humblefte forte,
That fometyme weare of Englandys progenye,
And haue theare bretherne fledde from Thy glorye,
For whome wee praye, as charytee dothe bynde,
Owte of the Feendys thrall Thowe wylte them vnwynde.

" Remembre wee theare, by many á daye,
Haue ferued Thy grace, as true Chriftyans ought,
And thorowe Thy mercye, we maye well faye,
Are hyther vnto endeleffe joyes brought :
To ceaffe their malyce let moue in Thy thought
At oure contemplation, O dreade Soueraygne!
To praife of Thy name to florifche ágayne.

" Remembre howe hundreadys remaynynge theare yeete
(Thoughe but an handefull to the reafydue)
Profternethe them downe as lowe at Thy feete,
In faftynge and prayinge to Thee that dothe fhwe,
Owte of their myferye them to refcue ;
Whois prayers attende, withe owres, in this cafe,
And call to Thy fowlde the ftreyed (by Thy grace).

" Remembre, the lengre Thowe ftayeft Thy hande
The ferdre they flee by numbres manyfolde,
Inowghe hathe fuffered the fewe that dothe ftande
Of wronges and fcoarnynges, as Thowe doifte beholde ;
Ouer Thy feruauntes the wicked are bolde,
And hathe (of malyce) mofte vyolentlye
Deftroyed and troadde downe Thy fanctuarye.

" Remembre the Cowntreys approxymat
At Englandys example howe they dothe flytt ;
No ferdre let them fo intoxycat
By ftandynge ftiffe in their fenfuall wytt ;
Put in their cheeakes Thy conftreynynge bytt
That will not approache Thy wyll to obey,
By meanys and foarfinges, as Thowe wotifte what wey.

" Remembre, if lenger Thowe lifte to forbeare,
Thy Chriftyan Faithe and godly reuerence
Wylbe abolifched vtterlye theare,
So ouer them hathe Sathan preamynence ;
Shewe furthe the powre of Thy magnyficence,
Let not Thyne Enemye that Royalme fo defpoyle,
And Thowe Cheeif Lorde of Royaltee and Soyle.

" Remembre, Thy name hathe floryfched theare longe ;
Their feruynge Thee theare, nowheare was the lyke ;
None had to Thy prayfe fo melodyous fonge,
In Europe, Afia, other Affryke,
Withe fweete enfence, as balme aromatyke,
Oratyons alfo of pure deuotion ;
Let thearfore of thém bee no dyuortion.

[*ſ.* 67.]   " Remembre Thy douaryes Thowe haſte them indude,
As *Beawtye*, *Wytt*, and *Aptnes* foueraigne,
Agilitee, *Boldenes*, and *Fortytude*,
Withe what maye decor Nature humayne;
Befydys their *Soyle* garnyſched withe *Grayne*,
And *Commodyteis* paſſynge to compare;
Suche noble Prouynce from Thee doo not ſpare.

" What if they hathe runne headelynge áwhile
For fynne, whiche Thowe haſte vnponyſched lefte,
Doo not foreauer Thyne Englande exile,
And ſuffre Thyſelfe to bee thearof berefte;
Agayne (as Thowe owghtiſte) bee Thowe thearin fefte,
For Thy great mercy, whiche none can dyſcuſſe,
And for the Bloodeſheadynge of Thy Sunne *Jeſus*."

Emongys whiche heauynlye Supplicatours,
The gloryous Queene of that highe regyon,
Withe ornat white virgynall awaytours,
In numbre manye, and fundry á legion,
In humbleſt wiſe that any maye thynke on,
For Englandys honoure and Chriſtian eſtate
The Syttynge in Throne ſhee dyd ſupplicate;

Sayinge, " O myghtye, and myghtyeſt of all!
Thowe, that of man art moſte myndefull alwaye,
Vouchefaufe olde Englande to grace agayne call
And dooe yt not from thy fauour delaye;
My *Douarye* it hathe beene many á daye,
By mynyſtrynge feruyce to the honoure of Thee;
Redreſſe the amyſſe to former degree.

" Geeue not the glorye of Thy holye name,
That theare hathe longe beene had in reuerence,
To anye other then to the felfe fame ;
Great mufte then bee the inconuenyence.
Graunte Reformation by thy Prouydence,
Thowe that (of mercye) defyreft to wynne
The fynner to grace, then perifche in fynne."

Thus maye imagyne eauery true harte
The Bleffed aboue for *Englande* to praye ;
So foone (of yt felfe) it cowlde not conuerte,
So farre and fo many weare gone á ftraye ;
Of whiche (as before) I cannot but faye
Oure godlye *Gryfilde* to ftreeke á great ftroake,
The mercye of God towardys vs to prouoake.

¶ *Heere are ſummed the great* Graces *planted in* Gryſilde *while ſhe was heere lyuynge ;* her highe Linage *myxte withe* Meekenes, *her* Pytee *to the pooare, her* Deuotion *to God, her* Sufferaunce in aduerſite, *her perfecte* Charytee *to all men, Fightynge agaynſte the* Worlde, *the* Dyuyll *and the* Fleſche, *whiche if theye bee* Martyrdoms, *then maye ſhe be likened for one.*

¶ *Caput* 20.

Her highe Progeny mixte withe meekenes moſte ſpecyallye.

OWE to ſome vpp the ſome of this purpoſe,
To glorye of God moſte ſpecyallye,
For ſpeciall graces, as I ſhall dyſcloſe,
In *Griſilde* planted moſte plentyouſlye ;
As firſte, her highe and noble Progenye,
Then her Meekenes and vertue foueraigne,
Seelden ſeene met in ſuche Eſtate mundayne.

[ſ. 68.]
Her lowly conſyderinge whearof ſhee firſte ſprange, as of the earth.

Seeleden ſeene Prynceſſe her looke to inclyne
Downe to the Earthe, as to bee but earthelye,
Whiche agaynſte fowle Pryde is cheif medycyne,
(Whoe liſte, geeue aduertence intentyuelye)
As dyd this *Gryſilde* for all her ſtate hye ;
Eauer ſhe had this ſpecyall reſpecte
To bee but mortall, withe ſynne all infecte.

Seeleden is feene Prynceffe as *Grifylde* was
Her Pryncelye iyen on the Pooare to conuerte,
Whiche was vnto her as myrrour or glaffe
Her orygynall to note in that parte,
As ofte reuoluynge in her inwarde harte
Howe God myght have fetten fuche in Eftate
And fhee (as they) to haue beene of like rate.

*her pytefull re-
fpectynge the
Pooare and In-
digent.*

Seeleden is feene Prynceffe the Pooare to vifyte,
And withe her owne handys the fame tapparayle,
But this goode *Grifilde* had cheeiflye delyte
The Pooare to helpe bothe withe meede and vytayle,
Whiche nowe (to her comforte) dothe greatly aduayle ;
Her meekenes (in that parte) to the Pooare adept
Chrifte, as to Hym felfe, Hee dothe it accept.

*her vifytynge
the Pooare and
helpynge the
fame.*

Seeleden is feene Prynceffe to fyt vppon kneeis
To God (withe the loweft) her felfe to commende ;
This humble woorkewoman as one of Chrifte Beeis
Agaynfte the hell Hornett did ftowtely contende,
Hoonye to Hys hyue to gather and to fende,
As fweete examples, which fhee dyd heere wurche,
To the furnyfchynge of His holye Churche.

*her humlinge
her felfe on
kneeis to God
in daylye
prayour.*

Seelde is feene Prynceffe to ryfe at myddenyght
On Dauyths harpe to fearche the melodye ;
This bleffed bodye had fpeciall delyte
In contemplation of that to occupye ;
Of God fhee purchafte great fauour thearbye,
As to witheftande temptations manyfolde,
And nowe in the Booke of Life is enrolde.

[*f* 63ᵇ.]
*her ryfinge at
mydde nyght
to ferue God in
contemplation.*

U

her meekelye
fufferynge in
aduerfytee.
Seelde is feene Prynceffe meekely to fufteyne
(In forte as fhe ought) this worldys vexation ;
This godly *Grifilde* to none did compleyne
But althynges tooke in goode acceptation,
Rather wifcheinge reconciliation,
By prayer to her Lorde omnipotent,
Then vengeaunce, plage, or other punyfchment.

her hie majef-
tie humelynge
wythe the
meaneft.
Seelde is feene ftate of magnanymytee
(As this goode *Grifild* was forted vntooe)
Feaffed with grace of pure humylitee
(As earfte is faid) with the meanefte to dooe,
Whois holye dooynges maye other (the lyke) wooe,
Meekenes, withe charytee, for to embrace,
As fhee, of God His fauour to purchace.

The Holy
Gohofte *was*
whoale her
ayder,
throughe
whome her
fame fhall
neauer dye.
Theis feeldome feene fightes in cheifly the mofte
In *Grifild* weare feene florifche floryfchelye ;
So was fhee ayded by the Holye Gofte,
As feelde in oure tyme was the like to efpye,
For which her highe fame fhall neauer fure dye ;
Thoughe heere Oblyuyon maye yt abrace,
So fhall yt not owte of the Better place.

[*f.* 69.]
Then ought this noble and godlye woman
To bee exalted in worthie degree,
For her life, that fo vertuoufly began,
Alfo contynued, as heere herde haue yee,
And lykewife ended, withe all charytee,
Wiche to conferre withe other bleffed
Withe like rewarde fhe is nowe poffeffed.

If wrongefull entreatinge and trobled harte
For ftedfaftely ftandynge in rightuoufnes
Bee a Martyrdome, by cowrfe of panges fmarte,
Thorowe Goddys woorkinge meryte to encreffe,
Then, as holye *Hierom* dothe expreffe   [Epift. 86,
Of *Paula* that clearly this worlde did forfake,   ad Euftoch.]
This *Grifild* maye in the numbre bee take.

Fightynge againfte theis ftowte Capytayns three,
The Dyuyll, the Flefche, and this Worldys vayne delyte,
Witheftandynge their meanys to iniquytee,
Whearto the Enemye the mynde dothe exite,
Á Martyrdome maye bee called fuche fight ;
Of whiche kynde Martyrdome, as I dooe geffe,
The lyfe of *Grifild* for her can expreffe.

But for it fittethe [*fic*] not oure facultee
Suche honor to anye as to impute
Of martyrdome, or fuche heauynlye degree,
Howe holye foeauer bee heere their brute,
Onlye the Higheft affignethe that fute ;
Thearfore to His appoyntement dyuyne
What Hee rewardethe to Hym wee refigne.

Remembre I doo this texte of *Salomon*,   [*f.* 69ᵇ.]
" Theare are in this life bothe godlye and wife   *Sunt Jufti at-*
Whois warkes withe God are in acceptation,   *que Sapientes,*
And yeat farre paffethe for Man to decife   *et opera eorum*
Whyther they ftande in fauour of Goddys iyes   *Dei ; et tamen*
Other yn hatred ; " for Hee onlye ys   *an odio dignus*
That all rewardethe after pleafure Hys.   *fit.*
     [Eccl. ix. 1.]

To whome all dowbtefulnes wee dooe commende
As to Hym that knowethe the hartys ſecreacye ;
In judgeing the beſte wee dooe not offende,
Sithe all wee referre to His dyuyne mercye
And to thaduauncynge of His powre myghtye,
For *Gryſilde*, and other, their vertues all
From Hym they ſprange, as well orygynall.

To Whome bee praiſe and exaltation,
Glorye and honour eauerlaſtyngelye,
Whoe graunte vs in this peregrynation
To lyue to His pleaſure accordyngelye,
As *Gryſildys* example dothe teſtyfie,
That, fynyſchynge heere a Chryſtian ende,
To reſte perpetuall wee maye aſcende.

Amen.

¶ *Heere endethe the Hiſtorye of* Gryſilde *the* ſeconde,
onlye meanynge Oueene Catharyne, *Mother to oure moſte
dread ſoueraigne ladye* Queene Marye, *fynyſched the*
25 *daye of* June *the yeare of owre Lorde* 1558 *by the
ſymple and vnlearned Syr* Wyllyam Forreſt, *Preeiſte,
propria manu.*

¶ To the Queenys Majeſtie.　

¶ *An* Oration *conſolatorye*
To Marye *oure Queene, moſte worthy of fame,*
That longe hathe traueyled in panges ſorye,
Nowe to quyet her ſelfe in Goddys *name,*

　　　¶ Wyllyam Forreſte.

MONGES muche inwarde profounde
　　perpendinges,
So ferre as ſeruethe wyttys perſpycuytee,
Twoe I adnote, before all other thynges,
To whome behouethe ſingular ſouer-
　　aigntee,
(Thoughe farre the *One* dyfferent in degree)
As of eache wearynge their recognyſaunce,
Looue, Honour, Dreade, and dwe *Obeyſaunce.*

Twoe are to bee obeyed aboue all thyngys.

The highe, myghty, moſte magnyficent Lorde,
That higheſt aboue holdethe pryncely reaſydence,
By Whome this worlde (ruynous) was reſtorde
To tholde forme and priſtynat preamynence,
The *Firſte* is, that cheeifly *Obedyence*
Withe thother Feualties are appropryat,
For that Hee is the Cheeif Pryncely Prymat.

God oure Creator moſte eſpecyallye.

Then nexte the highe Powre, oure ſoueraigne Queene. Thother art thowe, O ſoueraigne Prynceſſe!
Marye, Queene of Englandys domynyon,
So ſoarted by His omnypotent goodnes
That regnethe Three in perfecte unyon,
Yeat farre impar by juſte opynyon,
Thoughe heere in earthe nexte Hym I none alowe
So highe, woorthye, and noble, as art Thowe.

[ſ. 71ᵇ.] Honor, latria, dwe only vnto God: Honor, dulia, to men in their degreis. To yowe (I ſaye) dothe dygnelye appertayne
Moſte loyall duetyes for ſubjectes tenſue;
To God (the heauynlye myghty ſouerayne)
Honor, latria, to none other els dwe;
And to thee (Marye), as Clarkes can conſtrue,
Honor, dulia, thearby knowne to bee
Atwixte yowe twayne the great dyuerſitee.

God, Kynge Immortall, aboove; Mary, heere Queene mortal, beneath. Hee aboue, æuerlaſtyngly regnynge,
Thowe heere alowe, paſſible and mortall;
Hee in Hym ſelfe althynges conteynynge,
Thowe at His wyll to ſytt or to fall;
Hee omnypotent, Thowe but as His thrall,
Hee to commaunde, Thowe meekely to obeye;
Suche Hee, ſuche Thowe, thowe cannyſte not ſaye naye.

God, the creator; Mary, His creature. Hee the Lorde and Kinge; She His Mynyſtre. Hee God, That althynges created of nought,
And ſendethe the fruytes tencreaſe and to ſprynge;
Thowe His Creature, vpp traded and bought
Ouer His People to haue the gouernynge;
Thowe His Mynyſter, Hee thy Lorde and Kynge;
Thowe for thy Office to Hym comptable,
Hee alone Keyſor incomparable.

Hee Lorde, Thowe Subjecte; ſithe knowne ſo is *Hee*,
Hee thearfore, as Lorde aboue other all
Moſte paſſynge, highely magnyfied to bee
As *God* only, and Kynge Imperyall;
And *Thowe* aboue all creatures mortall
As His Electe and ſpecyall enoynted,
By Hym ouer vs to reigne appoynted.

To whome (that myghty magnyficent Kynge),
Beſydys all gracys Hee Englande can indwe,
Moſte ſpecyall cawſe of thankes renderynge
Wee ought to geeue, O noble Queene, for yowe,
For oure agayne reuocation nwe,
From Hereſyes wronge, dampnable and nought,
To bee in Chriſtyan eſtate agayne brought.

To bee created in ſorte heere humayne,
Withe dowaryes indued agreeinge to the ſame,
Of lyneamentes and wytt ſoueraigne,
Withe what els maye anye worthely name,
Concernynge in Faythe to bee owte of frame
(To heauynly paſſage whiche ordrethe the ſayle),
What maye theis all to purpoſe oughtes aduayle?

What maye yt profyte to bee as *Samſon* ſtronge,
Withe *Salomon* tafflowe withe wiſedome and wytt,
Withe *Neſtor* to haue heere contynuaunce longe,
Withe *Alexander* great in honour to ſytt,
Withe other worthyes whome Deathe made henſe flytt,
And to incurre eauerlaſtynge perdytion
For faylinge of true Chriſtyan relygion?

Howe late this Royalme by Scyſmys and Hereaſter was greatlye troboled.

So was ytt, it ys not yeate owte of remembraunce,
Moſte odyous Schyſmys this Royalme dyd late perturbe,
Almoſte the moſte parte geauynge attendaunce
(Aſwell of Nobles as the ruſtycall Scrubbe,
Withe thowſandys in Cyteeis and eke in Suburbe)
To that all true Chriſtian faythe dyd abhore,
Receauynge *plagys*, not yeat extynɗte, thearfore.

[ſ. 72ᵇ.]
God, for the Goodes ſake, ſended reſor- mation in this Royalme.

So heere contynuyng, by too longe ſpace,
Aboue (as I adnote) twentye yearys full,
Tyll God, of His meere and ſpecyall grace,
For the Goodys ſake reſpeɗted their trobull,
The cawſers (ſo cawſinge) withe ſorowes dobull
Owte of their romethes euacuatynge cleane,
Bycauſe they dyd them no better demeane;

Ereɗtynge then Thee, a Mayden well knowne,
(Thoughe cleane vnknowne concernynge mannys vſage)
By grace in thee that of longe tyme was ſowne,
Thowe to ſet free his *Churche* owte of bondage,
Whiche thowe not ſlackydſte, withe manly corage
Rather then womans, whoe liſte to aduerte,
For whiche harde corſayes hathe ſtreyned thy harte.

But bee aſſured in thy heauynlye Lorde,
For all thy Enemyes malignytee,
Howe eauer they ſpurne, or at thee remorde,
Hee wyll (as Hee hathe) from them defende thee,
Theyr ſtormys (I full hoape) ouer ſhaken bee;
Whoe anye moe ſuche wyll ferdre attempte
As had the other, God them not exempte!

Well thowe remembreſt (O noble woman !) *Tanquam*
The *Goode* God prouethe, as golde by the fyre, *aurum in*
And, conſequentlye, Hee fyndethe them than *fornace pro-*
Woorthye to haue Hys blyſſe for their hyre. *bavit electos*
Dauyd, whoïs harte Goddys ſpyrite can inſpyre, *Dominus.*
Declarethe the juſte to bee afflicted, [Wiſd. iii. 6.]
But God wyll them not ſee derelicted.

Vnto whiche purpoſe I thynke vpon well *Of the moſte*
Of godlye *Joſeph* the great perturbaunce, *chaiſte In-*
Sunne vnto *Jacob*, or *Iſrael*, *nocent* Joſeph,
Howe longe contynued his greuous peanaunce *ſunne to the*
Before eſtate quyet to hym dyd chaunce, *holy patriarke*
Whiche was from that hee was Sixteene yearys olde *Jacob, or*
Tyll nearehande Fortye, in Geneſis is tolde. *Iſrael.*

Hee was by Bretherne, curſed and enuyous,
Maligned, afflicted, vncharytablye,
Abanyſched farre from his Fathers howſe,
And ſolde (as bonde man) withe muche vylonye
Vnto worſhippers of ydolatrye, *So wryten by*
Steyde in the cytee *Indoculpitas* *Ephrem the*
Tyll haulfe yearys ende his byers dyd repaſſe. *godlye Gre-*

After, redeamed by monaye great ſummys
Into the howſe of the Lorde *Putyphrys*,
By meanys of his ladye hee thyther cummys,
Whois name *Memphytica* remembred ys, *So named in*
To the ende withe hym to commytt á myſſe ; *Joſephs Teſta-*
But hee recuſinge her luſte to content, *ment.*
Shee made hym to ſuffre impryſonement.

x

[*ſ. 73ᵇ.*] Whearwithe that Innocent helde hym pleaſed,
His cauſe commendynge to God æuerlaſtynge,
Fyndynge hymſelfe wondreſlye eaſed
From the temptation of fleſchely brennynge,
Rather contented, in pryſon lyinge,
Hys handys of that fylthe ſo clearlye to weſche,
Then daungerynge his ſowle by followinge the fleſche.

And thoughe in darkenes hee ſate deepe á lowe,
As abieðe (in this worlde) or caſte áwaye,
Withe Hym that the ſecreatys of hartys dothe knowe
Hee was in fauour moſte highelye (no naye),
And when Hee pleaſed to appoynte the daye
Hee fechte hym owte of the pryſon or dyke
And ſet in honour, as noman the lyke.

What highe
worthynes fol-
lowed goode
Joſeph after
aduerſytee

Hee ſet hym highe vpon *Pharaoes* ſteeade,
Withe annule on fynger, to ſigne or to ſeale,
Whois prudent prouydence the worlde dyd feeade
That els had periſched thorowe lacke of meale ;
No lyttle was the comforte hee dyd deale,
Suche wondreſull wiſedome in hym was ſownde
To foe and freende his grace dyd ſo abownde.

Hys worthynes yeat the worlde doth recowmpte,
Aſwell the Heathen as Chriſtyans true ;
For ſeruynge Hym, the Higheſt (that dothe ſurmounte)
Such ſingular wiſe can *Joſeph* indwe ;
And, as Hee *Joſeph*, ſo ſaye I vnto yowe,
O *Joſepha*, ſiſter vnto the ſame,
For hym reſemblynge as wee maye well name.

Hee was of bloode, natyuytee and lyne,   [ſ. 74.]
Of higheſt in this worlde trulye defcended ;
Noleſſe art thowe, thy tytle dothe defyne,
Of none on lyne to bee reprehended ;
At Sixtene yearys age thy greefes accended,
From that thy goode Mother her ſtate was put downe,
Ánd ſyns (moſte parte) thowe receauydſte thy Crowne.

For what cawſe was *Joſeph* maligned ſo
But for to his Bretherne he was contraryous ?
He, moſte earneſtlye, geauyn vertue vnto,
And in their doynges they eauer vicyous.
So, Badde at Goode are aye litigyous ;
Thoughe with the Badde the Goode can ſumwhat beare,
The Badde are farre of á contrarye leare.

Whye hathe maligned the Worlde agaynſte thee
(Ouer whiche the Dyuyll dothe ſo predomynat),
But for thowe woldyſte not of his aſſent bee,
Thy ſowle in his forte withe vice to vyolat ?
Suche on their owne headys dothe exagitat
Goddys indignation and ſcourge of vengeaunce
But they (in dwe tyme) pleaſe Hym by peanaunce.

What goode gote *Duddeley*, defrawdynge thy right,   *Of the Duke Duddelaye.*
Withe all that to hym weare aſſociat ?   *Of Sir Thomas Wyatt.*
What helped *Wyat*, that madde Beddelem knyght,
To foarſe his powre (by pryde) vnto *Ludgate ?*
Oather (of late) the forte inſanyat,
As *Henry Peckham*, with *Danyell* his feare,   *Of Henry Peckham.*
By falſe conſpiracye agaynſte thee to ſteeare ?

[ƒ. 74ᵇ.] Alas ! my harte euyn tremblethe withe in mee
To ſee of people the ingratytude !
O *Henry Peckham* ! howe happened thee
The Dyuyll withe ſuche blyndenes thee to delude,
Thy handys withe treaſon to bee ſo embrude,
Agaynſte thy Myſtreſſe to woorke ſuche pretence
Whiche loued thee, I dare ſaye in conſcyence ?

Thy Father ſo worthye and godlye a man,
Thy Bretherne alſo bothe Catholike and goode,
Thowe to degenerat, I merueyle than,
And yee (as to ſaye) of one nature and bloode ;
But (of olde ſayinge) happye is the broode
In whiche nother theeif nor vnthrifte dothe ſprynge :
Alas that on thee ſhoulde happen ſuche thynge !

Thowe, ſtandynge in trowthe (as true ſubieƈte ought),
Cowldiſte not haue wanted that was conuenyent,
For well I wote thy Myſtreſſe hathe in thought
Thy Father's ſeruyce, that was ſo euydent
In neadfull tyme, ere ſhee had regyment,
For his ſake tenderinge thy wealthe and woorſhippe
Tyll into deſtruƈtion thowe neadys woldiſte lippe.

[xviii. 2o.] But the father (*Ezechiel* dothe ſaye)
Shall not ſuſteyne the treſpaſſe of the childe ;
Thy wicked dooynges ſhall harme hym nowaye,
Hys fame ſhall floriſche, thoughe thowe bee exilde.
Why weare thowe peruerſe, why weare thowe ſo wilde,
Leacherous (ſome ſaithe) beſydys thy wedded wife,
Whiche, as others, hathe ſhortened thy life ?

Whoe withe his wife cannot bee contented
But wyll withe other his luſte ſatisfie,
As thoughe from Goddys lawe hee weare exempted,
Thoughe Hee not punyſchethe theare by and by,
He ſufferethe ſuche, as by thee dothe well trye,
To fall in ſome other abomynation,
So to receaue digne recompenſation.

Ceaſſe ſuche (I ſaye) as ſo yeat dothe practice,
Ceaſſe from ſo ſtoorynge Goddys indignation,
Ceaſſe from youre dyuyllifche cankered malice,
Ceaſſe from Conſpiracyes execration,
Ceaſſe from fowle Hereſyes incantation ;
For, withoute ceaſſinge from practicynges ſuche,
God will not ceaſſe youre myſeryes to tuche.

Howe the Dyuyll dare yee too dooe as yee dooe,
Agaynſte that that God wyll to entepriſe ?
Shee heere to reigne God is wyllynge theartoo,
And yee to the contrarye daylye deuiſe.
God will ; yee will not ; Wheare dothe this ariſe
But by the Dyuylles ſo inchauntynge your hartys ?
Ceaſſe from ſuche folye, and playe true mennys partys.

Youre dooynges ſeemethe for Religyons ſake :—
Curſed bee that Religyon, I ſaye,
That lycencethe men ſuche vyle wayes to take
Their headde to attempte and put ſo in fraye !
Dauyd Sauls cloake but clyppynge wheare hee laye
His conſcyence greuouſlye dyd remorde
For ſo tuchynge thanoynted of the Lorde.

[f. 75b.] But your Religyon attendethe moſte cheeif
(As well is knowne) to carnall lybertee,
Nuryſchinge manye á traytor and theeif,
Withe all kyndys of vyce that named maye bee,
And, as it is all voyde of purytee,
(Diſpleaſinge to God That ſittethe moſte hye)
So dothe it conduce to euyll deſtynye.

Yee may by your owne take euydent proofe,
And other by yowe if yee not deſiſte :
Clyme not ſo highe, vpp to the howſe roofe,
And ſodaynlye fall, your footynge beinge myſte ;
To late wylbe to ſaye then, " Had I wiſte";
Vſe yowe like ſubieꝃes, it ſhalbe ſo beſte,
For, " Bleſſed are they that lyuethe in reſte."

So hathe the wicked diſquyeted thee,
(O noble Queene!), as the like *Joſeph* dyd,
But *Joſephs* God, that thy vſynge dothe ſee,
(Whiche thy God is alſo, thoughe Hee bee hydde),
I fully ſo truſte wyll them nowe forbydde
Nomore to torment thyne innocent harte,
Bicauſe thowe ſuffreſt for takynge His parte.

Hee wyll them to ceaſſe by others quaylinge,
If eauer they mynde His fauour toptayne,
And thee to ceaſſe from inwardys complaynynge,
Bycawſe, as *Joſeph*, Hee can thee ordayne
To ſytt in ſtate moſte paſſynge foueraygne,
Aboue all *ladyes* as *Joſephe* dyd of *men*,
For that, as *Joſephs*, thy life in ſorte dothe ren.

So blowſterouſlye neauer hurlethe the wynde,   [ƒ. 76.]
Noather the ſalte ſeayes to rage and to rore,
But after great ſtormys cawlme weather wee fynde ;
Mennys malice alſ ſpett, then hathe they no more.
Wheare Trybulation (for Truthe) goethe before,
The Peace of God dothe certaynlye ſucceede,
As ſhall vnto thee withe æuerlaſtynge meede.

So prayethe for thee thy louynge Subiectes all,
And all true Chriſtyans I dare vndretake ;
What thoughe thyne Enemyes then frett at the gall,
God and the Goode ſhall for thy partye make.
Of this thówe maiſte aſſuredly make crake,
No noble bloode, that any oughtes can preeue,
Agaynſte thy Majeſtee dothe ſtoore or meeue.

And ferdre is to bee noted this thynge,
Of thy noble Counſelours the truthe to ſaye,
Neauer hathe beene ſeene to drawe by one ſtrynge
More ſtedfaſtely ſure then nowe at this daye,
Thy conference withe them they dooe it obeye,
For well they wote, as thynges withe the dothe happe,
Withe ſpeciall grace God dothe the rownde enwrappe.

To Subiectes (that true obedyence dothe meane)
To thynke theare vpon is ſpeciall comforte ;
So longe as the Nobles to thee dothe leane,
No paſſinge bee had to the Prauous ſorte,
But them to hamper or hawlter vpp ſhorte,
Nomore of them make, ſithe Lawe, Loue, nor Dredde,
From traytorous pretence their hartes can vnwedde.

[f. 76ᵇ.]
Inveni homi-
nem secundum
cor meum.
[1. Sa. xiii. 14.
Acts xiii. 22.]

Dauyd, that was fo contentynge Goddys mynde,
Seauyn fortes of Synners hee well dyd aduue,
Emonges whiche *false Rebellys* hee dyd owte fynde,
Whome vnto deathe hee not let to purſue :
As like authorytee reſtethe in youe,
So, wheare no Mercye can wynne them to grace,
After their defertes let Juſtice take place.

Suche are not worthye the Commone wealys wealthe
That by Rebellyon diſturbethe the fame ;
Whoe the Polycie vndremoynethe by ſtealthe
His recompenſation the Royalmys lawe dothe name.
Better Lawes rygour, á fewe fo to tame
(That will not them frame by dwe obedyence),
Then hundreadys to perifche for their lewde offenfe.

As Emendation charytee afkethe
Wheare Emendation dothe playnlye appeeare,
So Juſtice (of right) dwe penaltee tafkethe
Wheare malyfactours vngodlye dothe fteeare ;
Whearfore I wifche, in Cowntreys farre and neeare,
Chryſtyan obedyence in dwe forte to reigne,
That Charytee maye aboue Juſtice optayne.

Then fhall Goddys glorye florifche (as it ought),
Then fhall thy harte bee in quyet and refte,
Then fhall weale publike in right trade bee brought,
Then fhalbe althynges as wee can wifche befte,
Then fhall oure Kynge bee nomore as ſtraunge Gefte
But, as behoauethe, withe thee taffociat,
After oure longinge, iffue to procreat ;

Whois proſperous reuertynge from his countreye   [f. 77.]
Reioycethe the hartes of whoale your ſubieĉtes true ;
In ioye maye yee ioye, I hartelye praye,
Yearys longe and·manye ſo to contynue,
Iſſuynge betweene yowe ſuche worthye iſſue,
This Royalme to keepe from deſolation,
As beſt maye ſerue Goddys contentation,

And thowe theareof, ere God for the henſe ſende,
To ſee the perfeĉte Education,
After thy.trade, that it maye after bende
When thowe ſhalte chaunge this habytation,
In ſorte as thowe takiſte imytation
After goode *Gryſilde*, thy holye Matrone :—
So graunte the Lorde, that higheſt ſittethe in Throne !

¶ *Amen.*

APPENDIX.

SPECIMENS OF FORREST'S
OTHER WORKS.

I.

Hiſtory of Joſeph;

PART I: *His Troubles.*

[MS. Univ. Coll. Oxf. 88.]

It begins with the following Prologue :—

The Prologe *of* Wyllyam Forreſt, *ſometyme chapylayne to*   [*f. 2.*]
the noble Queene Marye, *yn the moſte famous Hyſtorye of*
Joſeph *the chaiſte, ſunne vnto* Jacob *the holye Patryarke,*
compoſed by hym in Balade royall (as appeareth), to the
glory of God and thacceptation of all goode Folke, he
humbly beſeachethe.

FF wyſedome hydde and treaſure ſaufe   *Sapientia*
   - vnſeene,   *abſcondita eſt*
                                    theſaurus in-
Off grounde inculte, ymployed to no   *viſus ; quæ*
                                      utilitas in
   good vſe,   *utriſque ?*
                                      Ecclus. xx. d.
Of thynges floriſchinge, pleaſaunte,
   freſche and greene,
Shut vppe, as the ſolytarye Recluſe,
Knowledge ſoueraygne thignoraunt to induce,
Monumentys ſuche in couert to retaynge,
To what any one breedethe ytt any gayne?

[ſ. 2ᵇ.]   This for induſtyon as thus I doo move ;
Wryters their warkes that leadethe vnto vertue
To keepe to them ſelues dothe not ſo behoue,
For then but them ſelues can thearof conſtrue,
None els profytinge ; ye ſee it for true ;
In publyke to walke, if it bee probable
To ſundrye mo yt maye be profytable.

This warke of *Joſeph* I then deteynynge
Vnto my ſelfe full foure and twentye yeearis,
Suche as it myght profyte thearof deceauynge,
Perhapps, as the meane, ſome honorable peearys,
In whiche my conſcyence partelye me ſteearys
That, as wee ought eache other to wyll well,
So this, to like ende, abroade to compell.

At whiche (ſuche wiſe) Goddys exitation,
Thoughe muche tedyous the olde to renue
Whiche laye roughe hewed, as dothe the maſon
His warke at the fyrſte let to contynue,
Tyll at more leaſure he geauethe yt forme dwe,
So I, accomplyſchynge warkys ſundrye,
For ſpace ſo longe ſayde let this warke lye bye ;

Tyll now (of late) withe my ſelfe aduertynge
It myght ſtande in acceptatyon withe ſome,
Thoughe other ſome it wronglye peruertynge
Of indygnation that happlye maye come,
When it ſhall abyde eauerye mannys dome,
[ſ. 3.]   The goode (I beſeache) to take yt in goode parte,
And the other—God mollyfie their harte !

For none ſo eauyn in ſuche weighty matter
Can hym behaue to trade his penne aright
But thearagaynſte may riſe ſome vayne clatter
Throughe ſome curyous, proude, enuyous wight,
Whiche (peraduentur) he takynge to wryte
Myght be founde to haulte ere he made an ende ;
So ſome can chalenge farre ſoaner then amende.

I wote this hathe not the floriſchinge veyne ·
Of *Gowers* phraſe, adorned in ſuche ſorte,
Oather of *Chaucers*, that Poete ſoueraynge,
To aſke their counſaylles I came all to ſhorte :
Lydgate in this gaue me no comforte ;
So tell I yowe, before yee doo ytt reade,
I cannot them rayſe, ſo longe ágoe deade.

But this maye ſerue for my excuſation ;
Not on fyne manchet eauery man to feede,
Breade but raunged ſeruethe to ſuſtentation
And doethe the neadye ſuffycientlye ſteede.
So this (my poore labour) in tyme of neede
May ſerue in readynge to be certyfied,
That els myght (happlye) be euyll occupied.

Whiche Hyſtory of *Joſeph*, ſo paſſinge wurthe,
Wolde to God ſome other, of farre fyner witt,
Had take vppon hym to wryte and ſet furthe, ·
As moſte worthelye myght thearto ſeeme fitte !
But ofte wheare clarkes ſuche thinge dothe pretermytt,
Foolys raſchelye entermedlethe their office,
As I (my ſelfe yeelde) in this enterpriſe ;

In whiche to ſome I ſhall ſeeme tedyous,
And chalenged for the prolixyte ;
In wrytinge a godde thinge I am thus curyous
To leaue not vnſayde that well ſaide may bee ;
Moreouer, I vſe heere this propertee,
What thynge of *Joſeph* to my handys chaunced
His Hyſtorye thearwith I haue aduaunced.

In placys I touche after my groſenes
The propertyes of the partyes pretence ;
What els ſhould I ? mee ſeemethe playne noleſſe,
Of joye or weepinge to grace ſo the ſentence ;
When the mateir treatethe of contynence
I handle yt as cummethe in my mynde,
And like ſo a whoare in her whoaryſche kynde.

I cannot call a jade a pawlferaye,
I cannot call a knaue an honeſt man,
But as the meere truthe happenethe alwaye
So harpe I thearon eauer nowe and than ;
Who can otherwiſe, let them that ſo can !
Flowres of Rhethoryke I gathred neauer one,
As of a pybble to make a preacyous ſtone.

¶ Finis.

*The conduɛt of Potiphar's wife, towards her hufband, is
thus defcribed:*   [*f.* 48ᵇ.]

" She had a cafte to caufe hym relent
Weare he neauer in fo fell á rage ;
Her woorde was to hym á commaundement,
She breeke hym fo at her firfte maryage ;
A heckforde fhe was, of the Dyuyllis parage,
Stande fhe cowlde and kycke (at her pleafure),
Her malyce myfcheuous had no meafure."

  Jofeph's Management of Potiphar's Servants.

More with a wóorde cowlde he of them gett   [*f.* 58ᵇ.]
Then, in his roometh, myght fome other tenne
Whiche cowlde· bothe cúrffe, blawle, [*fic*] fight and frett,
Whiche neadethe not emongeft honeft men ;
A dyfcreeyt Offycer nowe and then
Knowethe á meanys howe to perfuade
To wynne á knaue to an honeft trade.

Knaues to be handeled too knappyfchelye,
What (I praye yowe) dothe thearof ofte come
But thwartynge, hatred, and cankerde enuye,
To the áweye throwynge of no fmall fome ?
An olde fayinge ys, " A man of wyfedome
Withe gentle handelynge can bringe in frame
That by curryfchnes no twentye can tame."

Jofeph withe his folke no fuche waies wolde take,
Withe gentylnes he had them at his wyll ;
Well was he that myght doo for hys fake,
Although theyr burtheys ofte greued full euyll ;

z

Their wagys he wolde not longe keepe yn byll,
The deye of payment oanſe beynge preſent
They had theyr wages, witheout argument.

A poore man to labour, in heate or colde,
Yn weat or drye, howe ſo the weather bee,
Hauynge a wyef and a poore howſeholde,
Wythe chyldren, perhappys, one, twoe, or thre,
Suche to prolonge or defraude theyr duetee,
A dyuyllyſche propertee I maye yt call ;
Yeat ſo are poore folke ofte dealte wythe all.

[*f.* 59.] By no maner meanys wolde *Joſeph* doo ſo ;
Yf he had not monaye vnder hys lache,
To ſome honeſt frende he wolde then go
To haue (for the tyme) the Pooare to dyſpache.
Fye on all thoſe that dothe clawe and ſcrache,
Goodys to vpp hoorde all they maye come bye,
Hynderynge the Pooare muche fraudulentlye !

" The maiſter ought trulye hys wagys to paye,
The ſeruaunte (agayne) to doo his duetye,"
So wolde *Joſephe* to hys laborers ſaye ;
Yf in his abſence, as when he was bye,
They dyd not theyr deauer dylygentlye,
Woorſſe then Theauys he dyd them accownte,
And more before *God* their daunger dothe admounte.

Yeat, lyke an earneſt faithefull Offycer,
Leſte groſenes (of cuſtome) myght doo hynderaunce,
Specyallye wheare he ſawe moſte loyterer

Thear wolde he ſtyll be puttynge yn remembraunce,
Prayſynge other for their contynuaunce
About theyr labour, of purpoſe to brynge
To mende theyr ſlouthe by oother prayſynge.

An other propertye *Joſephe* dyd vſe,
Whiche hys buſynes furdered greatlye,
He wolde (thorowe ſlothe) at notyme refuſe
To ſaye, " O Searys, wheare are my maynye ?
Gawe, let vs towardys oure buſynes hye ! "
This woorde, " Gawe we," and goynge with them too,
Dyd ſix tymes more good then " Goo yee " ſhoulde doo.

*The Baker's, and a Fellow-Priſoner's Speech, in Priſon, after
Joſeph's Interpretations of his Dream :—*

" Fetche me ſome drynke, I praye the hartelye,
And alſo ſome meate, ſuche as wee ſhall haue ;
If I wyſte well I ſhoulde dye ſo ſhortelye,
I wolde of oure God á petytion craue,
To graunte ere I dyed to playe oanſe the knaue ;
By God avowe that I dooe truſte yn cheeif,
A mearye lyef yt is to bee á Theeif ! "

Sayde one that ſate theare next hym vnto,
" Weare yt not for hangynge ſo weare yt indeeade,
For yn that ſcyence I can as muche doo
As ſome other three for á great neeade ;
Oh ! howe we tryumphe when we doo well ſpeede !
Lorde, oather knyght, better cheare will not make
Then wee, when wee á goode bootvſe maye take ! "

" The weather boyſtorous withe wynde, ſnowe, or rayne,
Hayle, thunder, or lightnynge, or extreme froſte,
Theis all cannott make vs oughtys to refrayne
To ſeeke oure profyte to other mennys coſte ;
Who cummethe ouer late, let hym kyſſe the poſte ;
Oh ! what yt is (yn oure roauynge) to fynde
A bowchett, ſtuffed yn his naturall kynde !

" If wee ſpeede well, then fare wee of the beſte,
Wee drynke ſweete wynes to comforte the bloodde,
Wheare wee before tooke payne and euyll reſte
Wee playe and bankett withe other mennys goode ;
Wee laughe yt owte whyle theye chowe the cudde ;
Whyle they ryde and ſeeke to gett yt agayne,
Wee laugh them to ſcorne, to looſe and take payne.

[*f.* 93ᵇ.] " Wheare choarles doethe mocker and hooarde all vppe,
And cannot their goodys honeſtlye beſtowe,
Wee make huffaye cheere betweene canne and cuppe ;
What ſhoulde one dooe but playe the goode fellowe ?
Hee that á colde ys, let hym the coale blowe !
Lyttle preatye turls wee muſte mayntayne ;
As wee dooe ſpeeade, ſo ryſethe their gayne.

" Eauerye Arte his myſterye doethe enclude,
Of that and this to furnyſche yn dwe frame ;
Withe oure Facultee who ys oanſe endude
Muſte endeauer to excell in the ſame ;
Whoſe (emongeſte vs) moſte crafte can attaine,
As vynetyner to broache, other to inſtruĉte,
Hee ſhall as pryncypall bee then induĉte.

" The Doctours of Phyſyke or Aſtronomye
The nature of thynges to ſearche and to knowe
Are not more ſtudyous, I dare teſtyfie,
Then wee oure ſtudye lykewyſe beſtowe
To compaſſe what weyes the thynge maye followe;
Dooare, wall, ne locke, moſte craftely wrought,
Cannot witheſtande the contryue of our thought.

" Wee haue all Toolys that thearunto ſhall neeade,
Bothe Sawe, Fyle, and Chyſell, moſte pure and ſyne;
So can wee woorke, yf wee lyſte to take heeade,
That all his this deye to morowe ſhalbe myne.
Wee, that are mayſters cheyf of that Doctryne,
Clyentys abroade haue with geldynges to aſſyſte,
That can home ſpeede vs ere that wee bee myſte.

" If wee be take, oure necke verſe we can,
Whearbye we reacon to ſaue the necke bone ;
Hee that ſo cannot, ſome helpe muſte haue than
Too fee the Keeaper to ſcape the Pryſon ;
If the woorſte fall, then ys but a knaue gone.
What Foole ys hee, that for one houres hongeynge
Wolde leaue the lyfe to oure arte belongeynge ?"

Concluſion.

But for nowe this Booke ynoughe dothe ſuffice   [*f.* 97ᵇ.]
For one volume, as much remaynynge,
The reaſydewe of this treatyſe

Shall in another haue the ordaynynge,
After heauynes ſolace contaynynge ;
For heere endynge his great aduerſytee,
The next ſhall treate of his felycyte.

> *Heere endethe the tragedous trobles of the moſte*
> *Chaiſte Innocent*, Joſeph.

The Hiſtory of Joſeph.

PART II : *His Felicity.*

[MS. Royal Libr., Brit. Mus., 18 C. xiii.]

Dedicated to Thomas, Duke of Norfolk, K.G. ; with a
Prologue againſt Idleneſs. In the Dedication Alexander
Barclay is mentioned, in the following ſtanzas :—

NTO whiche ende, O worthye famous Duke!
A certayne wryter, Alexander Barkeley,
In eloquent ſtyle, all voyde of rebuke,
The booke of Mancyne in verſe did conueye,
Of Englyſche meater holdynge the weye,
Vnto the fower vertues cardynall,
To light mannys lyef, a lanterne ſpecyall.

And to your noble Graundſyer Thomas,
Duke, as yee are, of lyke tytle and ſtyle,
He dyd yt commende, withe ornat preface,

Yn forte the beſte hee coulde caſte or compyle,
Withe other warkes mo, to paſtyme fomewhyle,
Whiche noble Booke, as mentyon doethe leaue,
Moſte noblye, (withe thankes) he can them receaue.

Takynge egreſſyon in his noble name,
Receaued they weare in acceptation
For their worthynes and noble fame
In profytinge oure Englyſche nation,
Sought and upp bought, in buſye faſhyon ;
But nowe, not ſo, no inquyraunce for ſuche,
For idle playes are occupyed to muche.

I conſyderynge the veary truthe ſo,
And haue longe traveyled in lyke buſynes,
Althoughe my ſtyle doethe farre alooyf go
From Barkeleys, as the thynge ſelfe doethe expreſſe,
(Yeat not all voyde, to vertues encreaſe)
Was fully mynded in coarners myne to hyed,
As goode as abroade and not occupyed ;

Callynge vnto mynde yeat better aduyfement,
Your noble father, Earle of Surraye,
Howe (in hys tyme) to bookes he was bent,
And alſo endytynge manye a vyrylaye
In acceptatyon moſte highe at this daye,
Yowe, as of Bloode-condytion ſo by kynde,
In hoape thearof cleane altered my mynde.

II.

Verſion of Pſalms.

[Royal Libr., Brit. Mus., 17 A. xxi.]

To the moſt woorthie Prince Edwarde, Duke of Somerſet,
Uncle *vnto oure moſte dredde Soueraigne* Lorde Kinge
Edwarde the VI., *bee fauoure in God, withe honour and
peace in proſperous eſtate longe to contynue, ſo wiſchethe his
humble oratour W. Forreſte.*

F tymes the wrappinge and vnfoldinge to vue
Howe alterations commethe vnto paſſe,
The olde laide downe, preferringe the nwe,
For tyme nowe altrethe from tyme that ons was,
Tyme hathe not cauſe to complayne, Alas !
When thinges olde, inveterat and nought,
Are unto better alteration brought.

To argument the meanynge of my mynde,
In tyme to fore what vilenes haue we herde,
In ſonges and balades of veneryous kynde,
Before goode thinges much rather then preferde ;
As tyme that tyme ſuche blyndenes dyd regarde,
So our tyme nowe tyme otherwiſe dothe ſpende,
In godlye myrthe muche better to commende.

Inſteade of balades diſſonaunte and light,
Godly Pſalmes receaued are in place,
Conveyde in meatre of numbre and feete right
As vnto ryme apperteyneth the grace,
Sunge to the vyall, lute, treble or baſe,
Or oother inſtrument, pleaſinge to the eare,
With whiche commutation ought each man to beare.

The firſt that ſo endevored his payne
(As I haue herde, and perfeꝑlye doe knowe)
Was Thomas Sterneholde, by Atropos ſlayne,
The pyked beſte of all Pſalmyſters rowe,
Whois ſtepps dyuerſe attemptethe to followe,
And dothe full well, woorthye of highe prayſe ;
God contynue them in their godlye wayſe !

Excited thearbye (as the cockerell younge
After the olde to crowe as hee can),
The Pſalmes I haue heere entred emonge,
In followinge them my meatre to ſcan,
Thoughe lacke of knowledge my wittes dothe ſpan
Fynelye to frame them, as beſt may content ;
In doinge mye beſte I ought not bee ſhent.

Whiche Pſalmes I haue colleꝑed togither,
The names of whiche this proheme dothe enſue ;
The numbre of fyftie I haue brought hither,
Meatred by croſſe ryme, as dothe appeare true,
Bye eight and ſyxe, whoe liſte the ſame to vue ;
Which foarced me ofte to adde and to detraye,
To no hynderaunce of the ſenſe I dare ſaye.

If caſe I haue, (to my judgement vnknowne)
I will not ſtande in defenſe of the ſame,
But yeelde myſelf (by ignoraunce ouerthrowne)
To better learned, ſo to auoyde blame,
Rather then ſtyflye to ſtande to my ſhame ;
To envye anye I doe yt not mynde,
But in their vertue to followe ſome kynde.

For certaynlye this dare I holde and ſaye,
No better occupation can bee hadde
Then in the ſaide Pſalmes to ſinge or to praye,
Our man interyour to comforte and to gladde,
Conſyderinge greefes that maketh the ſame ofte ſadde,
As burthen of ſyn that foreſte dothe moleſte,
Remedye for which in Pſalmes is readye dreſte.

Oure carcaſes alweyes to feede and franke,
(As for the ſame cheiflye to carpe and care,)
It is to be compted but a mad pranke,
Sithe that ſo ſone takethe from hens his forthefare ;
The ſame then to pleaſe and leaue the ſowle bare
Theis Pſalmes forbyddethe, whoe lyſte taduerte,
And ſalve preparethe before the ſoare ſmarte.

And, for the vſage of wryters alweye
Is (as theye favour) to father their workes,
As dyd John Lidgate to noble Duke Humfreye,
So I (thoughe an ydyot, followinge clarkes)
Suche wiſe encoraged with their ſaide ſparkes,
To yowe, noble Duke, theis Pſalmes doe preſent,
As vnto whome my harte of love is bent.

Wheare other your frinds with giftes temporall
This Newe Yearis tyde your Honour dothe falute,
Wifchinge yow healthe and quyetnes withall,
And to withftande all falfe enemyes purfute,
I (befydes that) my prefent thus permute
With theis fewe Pfalmes, of fpirituall fee,
Wifche to your Grace æternall felycytee.

As Sternholde highefte in framynge of Pfalmes
Vnto the Highefte can deftynate his doinges,
Bicawfe I cannot fo highe reache the palmes,
Vnto meaner then dignyte of Kinges
(As vnto your Grace) I make my offeringes,
Befechinge the fame to take them in goode wurthe,
So fhall yee force me moe Pfalmes to fet furthe.

His verfion of Pfalm c. alone fhows fufficiently the
juftnefs of his felf-depreciation :*—

     " O all yee earthelye creatures
        In God (the Lorde) ioye yee
     Serve hym before all oother cures
        Withe all felycytee
     Before His prefence come ye yn
        With ioye and all gladnes,
     Clenfinge your hartes from deadlye fyn
        His favour to purcheffe
     Knowe yee the Lorde for He is God
        He made vs fenfytyfe

* The verfion in the old Englifh and Scottifh Pfalter is by Will.
Kethe. [See Rev. N. Livingfton's "Scottifh Metrical Pfalter," fol.
Glafgow, 1864, p. 28.]

So is His powre from owres far odd,
  Wee can geave nothinge lyfe.
We are the people and the fheepe
  Of His onlye pafture;
The weye into His gates ftreyte keepe
  With joye theare to manure
Rendringe vnto that heavinlye Lorde
  The prayfe of thankefgevinge
In hymnys that fweetlye dothe conchorde
  To fo noble a Kinge.
Prayfe ye His name, for fweete is Hee,
  His mercye fhall endure
For eaver in eternytee,
  So is His highe pleafure.

III.

The Governance of Princes.

[Royal Libr. Brit. Muf. 17 D. iii.]

With dedication, by "Sir William Forrefte preeifte," to Duke of Somerfet, to whofe victory in Scotland in 1547 Forreft thus refers :—

" S hathe not been herde, fo paffinge precife,
Withe the loffe of fivetie, or fewe moe certife,
XV thoufande for too confownde,
Miraculowfe it was : God was his grownde."

Commends him as a true Protector and faithful uncle.

The book prefented to him, that it may have his ap-
proval firft before it be given to the King.

The Table of Contents contains thirty-feven chapters,
but only twenty-four are found in the MS. There is a
drawing reprefenting the author as a young man in a
gown, with abundant hair, not tonfured, prefenting his
book to the King on his throne.

Advifes the King to found and endow fchools and
colleges. After dinner, to have mufic, or play at tables,
chefs, or cards, but at fedentary amufements only at night.

Advice about marriage :—

" A kynge Godde forbeade too bee nue fanglede,
His wief texchaunge for his luftis dalyaunce,"

and therefore he muft enquire beforehand " if fhee bee
entanglede ;" not to marry when infants, but that they
fhould at years of difcretion make " free election."* It
makes his "backe iche " to hear of a young girl marrying
an old man for money, or a youngling " an olde wiche."

Regulation of foreign affairs and commerce.

On choice of nurfes for children ; but, notwithftanding,
" What longethe to the nurcerye women paffeth mee."

Education ; judges ; impartial adminiftration of the
laws ; officers ; againft monopolies, regrating of grain,
accumulation of wealth ; need of protection of the poor
from encroachments of the rich. The King ought to
punifh all thofe who endeavour

" At ale howfe too fitt, at mack or at mall,
Tables, or dyce, or that cardis men call,
Or what oother game, owte of feafon dwe." †

* The reference here to the cafe of Henry VIII. is very evident.
† Quoted in Strutt's *Sports and Paftimes*, 1801, p. 245.

" *Out of feafon*" is on working days. Children to be
fent to fchool at four years old ; none to be fet to work
under eight; the fchool to be free in every town ; the
curate to teach them to fay, fing, and write, and to have
a honeft ftipend. An overfeer or controller to be appointed to punifh all idle perfons with the ftocks or
fcourging, and to have £3 or £4 a year out of the town
coffer, elected or re-elected yearly. The wool trade
ought to be encouraged. Proteft againft the grafping
avarice of the rich, and the raifing of rents and amaffing
of lands ; thofe who afk for the higher rent, and thofe
who give it, and fo turn out the old occupiers, fhall
alike go to the Devil. Rents ought to be kept as they
were forty years before. The poor man does not dare
to fpeake againft one who has the farms and abbeys, and
who will not give anything out of his " clampis," or he
will get " his hedde all to broken."

[*f.* 60ᵇ.] The poore man to toyle for two penfe the daye,
Some while thre haulfe penfe, orels a penye,
Hauynge wief, childrene, and howfe rent to paye,
Meate, clothe and fewell withe the fame to bye,
And muche oother thinges that bee neceffarye,
Withe manye a hungry meale fufteynynge,
Alas! makethe not this a doolefull compleynynge ?

The worlde is chaunged from that it hathe beene,
Not to the bettre but to the warffe farre ;
More for a penye wee haue before feene
Then nowe for fowre penfe, whoe lifte to compare :
This fuethe the game called *Makinge or Marre* ;

Unto the riche it makethe a great deale,
But muche it marrethe to the Commune weale.

To reyfe his rent, alas ! it neadethe not,
Or fyne texaƈte for teanure of the fame,
Fowrefolde dooble, it is a fhrewde blot,
To the great hynderaunce of fome mennys name.
I knowe this to bee true, els weare I to blame
To mooue this mateir in this prefent booke,
At whiche *Refpublica* lookethe á crooke.

A rent tò reyfe from twentie to fiftie,
Of powndis (I meane) or fhealingis whither,
Fynynge for the fame vnreafonablye
Sixe tymes the rent, adde this togither,
Mufte not the fame great dearthe bring hither?
For, if the fermoure paye fowrefolde dooble rent,
He mufte his ware neadys fell after that ftent.

So for that oxe whiche hathe beene the like folde
For fortie fhealingis, nowe taketh hee fyue pownde,
Yea, feauyn is more, I haue herde it fo tolde,
Hee cannot els lyue, fo deeare is his grownde ;
Sheepe, thoughe they neauer fo plentie abownde,
Suche price they beare, whiche fhame is to here tell,
That fcace the pooare man can bye a morfell.

Twoe penfe (in Beeif) hee cannot haue ferued,
Other in Mutton, the price is fo hye ;
Vndre a groate hee can haue none kerued,
So goethe hee (and his) to bedde hungrelye,
And rifethe agayne withe bellies emptie,

Whiche turnethe to tawnye their white Englifch fkyn,
Like to the fwarthie coolored Flawndrekyn.

Wheare they weare valiaunt, ftronge, fturdy and ftowte,
To fhoot, to wraftle, to dooe anye mannys feate,
To matche all natyons dwellinge heere abowte,
As hitherto (manlye) they holde the chief feate,
If they bee pinched and weyned from meate,
I wiffe, O Kynge, they (in penurye thus pende)
Shall not bee able thye Royalme to defende.

Owre Englifche nature cannot lyue by rooatis,
By water, herbys, or fuche beggerye baggage,
That maye well ferue for vile owtelandifche cooatis :
Geeue Englifche men meate after their olde vfage,
Beeif, mutton, veale, to cheare their courage,
And then I dare to this byll fett my hande
They fhall defende this owre noble Englande.

Labourers' wages fhould be raifed from $1\frac{1}{2}d$. a day
to 6*d.* in the fhorteft days, and 7*d.* and 8*d.* as the days
get longer, working truly and diligently.   Thoufands
would get wed had they houfes " to coauer their hedde."

Defcription of kingly virtues.   Thofe who have been
maimed in war ought to be provided for.   Some one
ought to be employed to go about amongft the people
and hear all that is faid againft the king.

At the end of the table of contents is this note, but
the promifed narrations are not found in the book :—

" At thende of this warke fhall enfue certaine narrations exemplifinge fundry of the maters of the aforefaide
tytles."

IV.

Life of the Blefsed Virgin.

[Harl. MS. 1703.]

ORREST mentions in this poem that a leafe had been granted by a College,

" . . . . the name I put bye,
Of whiche the tytle went in our Ladys name,"

omitting the title of our Lady, confequently the leafe was declared void and of no value, and the farm forfeited. In " this prefent yeare 1571 " he faw a letter written from the " cheeif partye," now " farre higher " in office, in which he dated fuch a day after "thannuncyation," difdaining to fay " of oure Ladye." For forty years together, from 1532, the Blefsed Virgin has been blaf- phemed ; *e. g.* a prieft at an alehoufe fitting on the ale- bench, faid fhe was no better than his wife (rather, his concubine), and compared her to a faffron bag ; as foon as our Lord left her womb, fhe ceafed (like a bag emptied of its contents) to be any better than any other woman ; but upon leaving the houfe he fell down dead. Second inftance ; a woman born in mean eftate, raifed to a high one, of diffolute life, who more than others made herefy

B B

to ariſe and flouriſh in the land [Anne Boleyn?]; her
time was ſhortened by "the chief," by divine ſentence.
Third inſtance; an acquaintance of the writer's, who had

> " Syngular knowledge in muſyk's ſcyence
> So that his fame, ſyngularlye alone,
> Over this Royalme in ſpecyall pryce ſhone."

He had written many ſongs in praiſe of the Bleſſed
Virgin, many of which remain, but no ſin that he had
committed grieved him ſo much as theſe.   He died mad,
after having been ſo for two years.   Fourth inſtance ;
a woman at Mancheſter was in the habit of comparing the Bleſſed Virgin to a ſaffron bag; ſhe died of the
yellow jaundice.   Fifth inſtance ; a man the writer knew
well, ſtrong, athletic, hearty, who always reviled the
Bleſſed Virgin, notably at a barber's when he once went
to be ſhaved ; he, when fifty years old, became decrepit,
weak, dirty, and loathſome to behold.   At Chriſtmas,
1545, the writer was invited to go to a Knight's houſe of
much eſtimation, where Miſrule, in hereſy, whoredom,
ſwearing, and the like, went on all the year ; there he
did his beſt with ſong and organs to celebrate ſervice in
the chapel; but while ſinging an anthem one night
there came in a gentleman, as they called him, and a
ruffian, and ran into the choir, and kneeled down on the
ſtones, and ſang, "Ave Maria, gracy plena, Dominus
drinke onys," and then got up and departed; the firſt
was afterwards ſlain, and the other drowned.   Many
now think nothing of any authority that is not in Scripture :—

" To fyne me thynke fuche curyofite ;
Bycawfe my name in Scripture not expreft,
Ergo, my name not Wyllyam Forreft."

Account of the beginning of the Feaft of the Conception in William the Conqueror's time, out of "owre
olde pamphiles."

Prayer to the Bleffed Virgin and to God to help
againft Luther's herefy ; but the author prays alfo for
" owre noble Quene here," [Q. Eliz.], and continues :—

" For one man, the Buffhoppe of Rome (I doe meane),   [*f.* 76.]
Let not Chryftes Churche fuche myferye fufteyne
As to conculcat and ouerthrowe cleane,
Sithe yt their partyes rather to mayntayne
In eauery Royalme, as thus to ordayne,
As James and the reft had placys by name,
So in eache countreye a buffhoppe foueraigne
To haue and to doo in chardge of the fame.

Of me a member of Chriftys Churche fo,
Grounded on Faythe, Hoape and true Charyte,
Suche my defyer withe all Chryftyans mo
To fee her floryfche in peace and vnyte."

At f. 85^b is the following interefting ftory relative to
Alexander Barclay :—

One, on a daye, in companye
Chaunced to faye thus fodaynlye,
" I yeafter daye was in daungere
Of necke breakinge in a mannere ;

My mare fhee ftumbled adowne right
That I fell to the grounde then quight,
But, thankes too God and oure Ladye,
I caught (at all) noe harme therebye."
"Whye," fayde there on then of the Garde,
" The matter dyd yt goe fo harde,
That God's helpe there might not affifte
Although oure Ladyes had ben mifte?
Ye derogate much God's glorye,
For which yee maye bee right forye.
In ignorance yee bredd all waye,
Therfore yee wotte not what yee faye;
Some punyfhment God fende ere longe,
That yee may knowe what right, what wronge."
An other dyd replye forth waye,
Called Alexander Barkeleye,
Then fittinge there other amonge,
And to the Cowrte dyd eke beelonge,
Who was much fyne and eloquente,
And could tranflate and eke convente.
In Poetrye, other Scripture,
Emonge vs yeat are well in ure
His workes fundrye which I haue redde,
And yeat doth live though hee bee dedde,
Which certaynly fo well are pende
That none this deye can them amende.
Which Alexander Barkleye than
The matter take in hande hee can,
And fayd, " No harme was in fo fayinge,
By good reafon thus approouinge ;—
I doe remember three yeares paft

Yee dwelt at Croydon, fure and fafte,
With fuch a man, I knewe you well,
Wherfore I can the better tell.
A longe lubber yee were in deede,
Much flovenly yee ware youre weede,
With coate of lethere, paltocke wyfe,
Youre hofe lyke fo in floven wiffe
Pachte upe unto the myddle legge,
Youre fhooes beedobbed with nayle and pegge,
And ofte to London yee carryed coales,
Youre hatte beefrett with fundrye hoales.
Who fhoulde haue fought fyve myles aboughte
Coulde not haue founde a veryer loute.
But for yee were bygge, longe and talle,
Thankes bee to God now, firft of all,
And to Kinge Henrye fpeciallye,
As the truthe by you doth now trye,
Who of his grace hath you preferde
To bee a Yoman of his Garde,
And doo become youre wearinge well;
But playnely, further forth to tell,
If Kinge Henry, though poure farre odde,
Had not putt to his helpe with God,
It might bee fayde and allfo fworne
Yee hadde continued as beforne.
Therfore in naminge oure Ladye
No harme, then naminge Kinge Henrye.
God without theyre affiftance can
Doo what Him lyfte, who lifte to fcan,
Yeat, by Saint Pawles authoritye,
Godes helpers in fome thinges wee bee.   [1 Cor. iii. 9.]

The plowe man but hee ſtyrre and ſowe
No corne or grayne is like to mowe,
Yeat dare I ſaye in everye preaſe

[1 Cor. iii. 7.] God onlye geveth the encreaſe."
The Yoman of the Garde dyd yealde,
As on ouercome in the feelde.
Barkeleye was boulde to ſaye his mynde,
For hee in Courte had manye freynde;
The matter then turned to ieſte,
They eate and dranke; all was in reſte.

At f. 100 is, "A dyttye or ſonet made by the Lorde Vaus in time of the noble Queene Marye, repreſentinge the Image of Deathe."

The Dict. of Nat. Biography, but Catherine of Aragon, says that the first child was christened Henry; he lived only a few weeks (Jan'y, 1511—Feb. 22. 1511). I must [seem to] have confounded this child with another, the brother of Henry VIII + 1502. It was to this Arthur that Catherine was first married. ...

NOTES.

"*And, to name,* Arthur *(certaynelye) had bee.*"—P. 39.

NOTWITHSTANDING the apparent certainty with which this is ſtated, our author appears to be in error in thus giving the name of Arthur to Henry's firſt child. He is called *Henry* by Sanders, with whom all other hiſtorians agree.

"*In Latyne, Frenche and Spaynyſche alſo.*"—P. 44.

The Princeſs Mary's French teacher was Gilles Guez, Duwes, or Dewes, who printed his inſtruction-book under the title of *An introductorie for to lerne to rede, to pronounce and to ſpeke French trewly, compyled for the right high, exellent and moſt vertuous lady, the Lady Mary of Englande.* This, which went through three editions in England, was reprinted in 1852 in the great French *Collection des Documents inédits.* It contains various converſations ſuppoſed to have been held by the tutor and others with the Princeſs at various times, together with letters and verſes, which tend to ſhow the amiable temper of Mary and the friendly relations which ſhe held towards thoſe around her.

P. 47. The "ymage" here mentioned does not appear to have been ſet up as a wayſide crucifix, but to have been in a wayſide chapel. Stowe, in his *Survey of London,* when ſpeaking of Goſwell Street and the ſuburb without Alderſgate, ſays, "There is at the fartheſt north corner of this ſuburb a windmill, which was ſometime by a tempeſt of wind overthrown, and in place thereof a chapel was built by Queen Katherine (firſt wife to Henry VIII), who named it the Mount of Calvary, becauſe it was of Chriſt's Paſſion, and was in the end of Henry VIII pulled down, and a windmill newly ſet up as afore." (Edit. 1842, p. 160.) The ſpot is ſtill known as Mount Mill; it is in the pariſh of St. Luke.

P. 60. Sanders relates that reports were prevalent that Wolſey had poiſoned himſelf, and an aſſertion to this effeċt was interpolated in the early editions of Cavendiſh's Life of the Cardinal. But here we have the teſtimony of one who was likely to be thoroughly well-informed in the matter, that the cauſe of death was an over-doſe of medicine, which would eaſily give occaſion to the ſtory of poiſon. It is curious to find from the *State Papers* that Wolſey had in years paſt been in the habit of over-phyſicking himſelf. In a letter written in 1519, Sir T. More tells him that the King ſays Wolſey may thank him for his health, becauſe by the King's counſel "ye leave the often taking of medicines that ye were wont to uſe." (Vol. iii. part 1. p. 154.)

P. 73. It is from Cardinal Pole that we learn that the original ſuggeſtor of the aſſertion of the Royal Supremacy, whoſe name Forreſt ſo carefully ſuppreſſes, was Cromwell. Pole gives a report of Cromwell's addreſs to the King which cloſely agrees in ſubſtance with that in the text. (*Apol. ad Car.* v., pp. 118-22, 125-6, vol. i.; *Epiſt. Poli*, 4°. Brixiæ, 1744.)

P. 111. Mr. Froude refuſes to believe on the authority of Cardinal Pole that Henry would not grant leave to Queen Katharine to ſee her daughter when on her death-bed, and does not think it poſſible that permiſſion was aſked. But Pole's (only too-probable) account is fully confirmed by our text, which repreſents the Queen as ſaying that it was forbidden, without reaſon aſſigned, that ſhe, the dying mother, ſhould take leave of her daughter. And we have been before told (at p. 85) that it was a dangerous thing for any one to convey letters on either ſide.

Pp. 155, 156. Little mention is made by hiſtorians of the conſpiracy in which Henry Peckham, ſon of Sir Edmund Peckham, was involved. His confeſſion, preſerved in the State Paper office, under date of 9th December, 1556, ſtates that its objeċt was to ſend the Queen over the ſeas to her huſband, and to raiſe Elizabeth to the throne; he was himſelf led to join in it by the ſolicitations of Chriſtopher Aſchton, who repreſented to him that the Queen was the " vnthankfulleſt myſteres on the earth, for ſche hathe gyuen thee but one hundered marks a year, and hathe taken from the foer." The Earl of Weſtmoreland and Lord Williams were implicated, and Sir Henry Dudley was ſaid to have engaged all the gentlemen in London that were ſoldiers. The only full account of the conſpiracy is to be found in Mr. J. Bruce's *Verney Papers*, Camd. Soc. 1853, pp. 59-75.

GLOSSARIAL INDEX.

*BANYSCHED*, ban-
ifhed, 153.
Ablaɓation, weaning,
43.
Abrace, to, to rub out,
to efface, 146.
Accended, kindled, 155.
Accloyd, clogged, overloaded, 92.
Adept, acquired, 145.
Adnote, to, to notice, 3, 35, 96, 123,
149.
Advayle, to, to avail, 145, 151.
Aduue, to, to fee, notice, 160.
Affayde, affeɓed, 43.
Alleaued, allowed; five wives " al-
leaued " to Henry after Q. Katherine,
133.
Alowe, a lowe, below, 134, 150, 154.
Alowde, approved, 46.
Alter, other, 131.
Amate, difmayed, 95.
Amyddys, amidſt, 121.
Apayde, fatisfied, pleaſed, 101.
Applyaunt, united, attached, 35.
Attoanſe, at once, 56.
Avowe, to, to vow, 171.
Avoyd, to, to quit, 92 ; to remove, 96.
Awaytours, attendants, 142.

Beedobbed, beefrett, ornamented all
over, 189.
Bebote, to, to promiſe, 96.
Bequeaue, to, to bequeath, 104.

Blanked, paled, 95.
Blowſteroufly, bloyſteroufly, boifteroufly,
109, 159.
Bonarly, pleaſing, 27.
Boote, remedy, help, 57.
Bowchett, a budget, a travelling-bag,
172.
Brute, report, 30, 147.

Carpe, to, to talk, 178.
Certiſe, certainly, 180.
Cheaue, obtain ; " hee fhoulde euyl
to-cheaue," he fhould utterly obtain
evil, 77.
Childred, children, 131.
Choarles, churls, 172.
Chriſtianed, chriſtened, 42.
Clampis, clutches, 182.
Clokedlye, obfcurely, 130.
Coarſye, coarſey, corſaye, vexation, 33,
96, 152.
Cockerell, a young cock, 177.
Cocking, fwaggering, boaftful, 81.
Conſtellation, the ruling planet of one's
life ; " tooke in goode worth her
conftellation," 101.
Convent, to, to make to agree (faid of
a tranflation agreeing with the origi-
nal), 188.
Couraged, took to heart, 15.
Crake, a boaft, 159.
Culpate, to, to involve in evil, to make
faulty, 3.

C C

INDEX OF NAMES.

THE END.

CHISWICK PRESS: PRINTED BY WHITTINGHAM AND WILKINS,
TOOKS COURT, CHANCERY LANE.